No Regrets in Serena Cove

Serena Cove Silver Romances 3

Lynne M. Spreen

For Bill – my sweet husband, my mentor, and my best friend.

No Regrets in Serena Cove

Serena Cove Silver Romances 3

Lynne M. Spreen

One

Sunlight danced off the water, the Pacific Ocean stretching wide and blue below the bluff. From up here, the waves were all flash and movement, their roar softened by distance. A line of pelicans glided past, low and smooth as stones skipping the surface.

But not everybody was enjoying the view. In fact, JoLynne Coltrane realized she was gaping like a fish at a perfectly nice man she never expected to see again.

He stood tall in the doorway on the patio deck of their community clubhouse, waiting for her to say something. Lean, weathered, with salt-and-pepper scruff along his jaw. That old, broken-in denim look, with broad shoulders and good hands.

Seeing her staring, he broke into a smile, slow and easy. His hair was shorter now. She remembered it longer, a little unruly.

"Hey there," he said, voice warm. "Hope I'm not interrupting."

She lifted her chin.

"Beau," she said.

"It's been a while, hasn't it?" he said. "How are you? I was at the funeral, but we didn't get a chance to say hello."

JoLynne nodded. She remembered him that day, how he'd stood back respectfully with some other guys from the warehouse where her late ex-husband had worked. At the time, she'd kept to herself as much as possible, her sister Vivian shielding her. Acting like she was protecting the grieving widow, when JoLynne just wanted it over with.

Beau's voice reached her again. "I've been meaning to stop by and see how you're doing. I thought maybe we could catch up. Have coffee or something." He held out a brown paper bag. "Also, I have something of yours."

JoLynne stared at the bag, not really seeing it. There was something about him. The way he stood there, quiet and certain. Unassuming. It brushed against something she'd put away a long time ago. A memory of a place, a sense of something lost. The scrape of boots on dry earth. Sunlight on flannel. Arms resting on a fence rail, the wood warm under her elbows.

Jesus, get a grip. She shoved her chair back and stood up. "Let's go for a walk."

The door closed behind them as he followed her out of the clubhouse office. "There's a bench on the bluff. We can talk there."

"It's quiet here," said Beau, his voice deep and rich. It reminded JoLynne of the ranch, of the men and their no-nonsense way of speaking.

"It's a graveyard," she answered.

They fell into step on the sidewalk leading to the scenic viewpoint.

JoLynne glanced back at the clubhouse patio, but an overgrown bougainvillea shielded them from any prying eyes. That was good. Gossip traveled fast in her small community, a modest mobile home park in an ideal location that had somehow resisted upscale development.

Beau was waiting for her to sit, so she did, and then he joined her. At their feet sprawled the vast ocean, a carpet of sparkling blue reaching all the way to Asia.

"Awesome place to live," he said.

"It can be."

"If I lived here, I think I'd sit on this bench every day." He looked at her, eyes hidden now behind his sunglasses. "You know that Tokyo is almost a straight shot that way?"

She shrugged. "I guess. I mean, I know Japan is on the other side of the Pacific."

"More than that," he said. "LA and Tokyo are almost on the same latitude."

JoLynne gave him a wry smile. "Folks, meet Beau Landry, world geography specialist."

He laughed, and she stared at him. The man was absolutely golden. He radiated happiness somehow.

Still, her curiosity was killing her. She cut a glance toward the bag, wondering what was in it.

Beau was smiling. "You remembered my last name."

"Gene might have mentioned you a time or ten," said JoLynne. "He thought you were a hotshot."

"But in a good way, right?"

JoLynne turned her head. In fact, Gene had been bitter about Beau, the way he'd come up so fast, passing over the older guys to take over management of the logistics facility where they worked.

"He liked how you kept the warehouse," said JoLynne. "Said you were smart."

"Don't know about that," he said, "but I am a logistics nerd. You have to be in my job."

"Oh, right," she nodded. "Ships and ports. Got it."

He tapped his temple with one finger, acknowledging her brilliance. She smiled, almost bumping his shoulder before catching herself. She barely knew the guy, really.

"Okay, Poindexter. What's in the bag?"

Beau gave her a funny smile. "I loved that show."

"You're not old enough."

"You'd be surprised," he said. Then his smile faded. "After Gene left, we did some renovating of the employee breakroom, lockers, that whole area. And we found something Gene must've left behind."

He handed her the paper sack, his face a study of discomfort and apology.

She took it and opened it. Inside was a picture frame. When she pulled it out and looked at it, she caught her breath.

The photo was of her, a young JoLynne on horseback, sunlit and strong. She looked up, her heart heavy. "He had this in his locker?"

"That's what the construction people told me."

JoLynne bent her head, angling the framed photo away from the sun. "I remember this day," she said, almost to herself. "I was a teenager, and they let me compete at the rodeo. Barrel racing. I took second place. It was one of the best days of my life, but then also, the worst."

She looked up at him. His eyes were the most arresting color: green, with shards of hazel, but what killed her was the look of sympathy there.

No, no, no. Not going there. She started to thank him and get up.

But he kept talking. "Being a kid with horses, that's the best childhood somebody could have. My opinion."

She sat back down. "It was pretty great."

"Do you still ride?" he asked.

She shook her head. She hadn't ridden since leaving Montana decades ago.

"Why not, if that's not too personal?"

That voice again, so warm and gentle. It annoyed the hell out of her. She scoffed, trying to bluff her way past the feeling. "Life, you know? I've been busy with life."

"Man, I hear you." Beau leaned forward, resting his elbows on his knees, gazing out at the water. "I don't know if you're aware," he said, "I live on a ranch. My brother and I. We're out in Ramona, not too far if you'd like to ride sometime. Just let me know."

JoLynne stared out to sea. Boats of all sorts plied the blue, and in the distance, a freighter headed west. She swallowed hard.

Yes, she wanted to say. Yes, I would love to ride. But she hadn't been on a horse since that horrible day, and she wasn't about to start now.

She stared at the picture. It was too much. Too much. Her eyes stung, in danger of spilling over.

"Thank you." She stood up, glad to be wearing sunglasses. "I need to go."

He leaped to his feet. "Is everything okay?"

"Fine, fine. I just need to go. Thank you again for this."

With that, she spun on her heel and hurried back to the parking lot, jumped in her golf cart, and drove away, leaving Beau standing on the lawn by the clubhouse.

Pulling into her driveway, holding the wheel with both hands, she let her head fall back, closing her eyes.

On the day of the picture, she'd been the top person on their high school team. She'd come in second, about to burst with pride, only to have the neighbor come get her and face the tragedy at home.

"You taking a nap or what?" Her sister's voice cracked at her from the porch.

Shaking it off, JoLynne climbed the steps. "Are you done packing?"

"I'm ready to leave, just waitin' on you," said Vivian, dramatically looking at her watch. "Don't know why you even bother to keep this place. Just get a condo by me and we can be gone all the time."

JoLynne smiled. "I'm not like you, Vacation Barbie."

They laughed, easy with each other after all the years of ups and downs. Her sister had married well, if not happily. After disembarking the ship in San Diego, Vivian had been staying with JoLynne for a few days before returning to her fancy but lonely home in Pacific Palisades.

"What's in the bag?" she asked.

"You'll never believe this." When JoLynne took out the picture, Vivian covered her mouth. The two sisters stood shoulder to shoulder, remembering. The two of them were silent for a bit, lost in thought.

"Weird how it comes back after so long," said Vivian. "Half a century and you remember it like it was yesterday."

JoLynne took the picture back, holding it facedown.

"Where'd you get it?" asked Vivian.

When JoLynne told her, Vivian perked up a little. "His name's Beau? I bet he's handsome. What's he look like?"

JoLynne scowled. "Your imagination just never quits, does it."

Vivian persisted. "Is he single? Does he have a nice shape?"

"You horn dog. I have no idea."

"You've got eyes, don't you?"

"He's definitely good-looking, but I don't know if he's single." She thought for a minute. She hadn't seen Beau with anyone at the funeral. "I think he might be. He invited me to come ride horses with him at his ranch."

"Oooh," Vivian squealed. "Did you tell him you would?"

"Not exactly," said JoLynne, remembering how she'd run off with hardly a goodbye.

"You need to get moving," Vivian said. "Good lookin' single man running around—that ain't going to last. You call him back and tell him you're ready to ride." She waggled her eyebrows.

"Shut up," said JoLynne. "I've got my hands full without some guy to bother me."

The two sisters shared a hug.

"This was great, but maybe next time, you'll have an actual bed for me," said Vivian. "That fold-out couch is going to kill me yet."

JoLynne stood on the porch, waving as Vivian drove away. She was lucky to have her sister in her life, and she knew Vivian felt the same way. Being able to travel together now was a boon for them both.

On the cruise ship, JoLynne and Vivian had taken a dance class and a cooking class, watched the sun come up in the morning and go down in the evening, enjoyed a massage and facial, and come home with goodies from the shipboard gift shop.

It was just such a relief not to have to be constantly listening for a voice crying out for help, to be counting out pills or ordering oxygen tank refills, or all the other things she'd been doing for the better part of the last three years.

But when Gene, her ex-husband, had come dragging his ass up on her porch that fateful winter day, JoLynne heaved a big sigh, took him in, and nursed him until he died. She might be stupid about men, but it was the right thing to do, and she would never regret it.

Inside, the house was cooler than she had expected. She dropped her purse by the door and set the photo on the counter. Heading to the fridge for a bottle of water, she spotted her post-caregiving list still tacked up by a cruise ship magnet, the one shaped like a tiny life preserver. The list said:

BE MORE SOCIAL
• Join a club
• Go dancing
• Try online dating (??)
• Get involved with park
• Reconnect with old friends

At that last one, she rubbed her forehead. When Beau gave her the photo, she'd been borderline rude. He hadn't known it would trigger her.

She took the water, shut the fridge door, and lingered, leaning against the counter. She ran a thumb along the water bottle label. At the very least, she owed him an apology. Maybe apologizing counted as being social.

She'd get to that in a few days.

Maybe.

Two

Well, that was a kick in the head.

After work that afternoon, Beau did his usual barn chores, feeding and spending time with the three horses. He brushed Buck, thinking about how JoLynne had taken off the moment she saw that picture. He could tell it meant something to her, so even though it got her upset, he was still right to give it to her. What else could he do, toss it?

Even before he gave her the framed photo, he had spent maybe a few too many minutes studying the black-and-white, sun-faded image of JoLynne in her teens, standing beside a horse on her family's ranch in Montana. Work-worn jeans, no makeup, a loose braid, a big smile. She looked strong and steady, reins in one hand, the other patting the horse's nose.

He felt the same way around his own horses, and his ranch, which made him feel as if they knew each other. That was idiotic. He'd only seen her when she was with Gene at company picnics and the like.

Beau had to admit he went over to her place thinking he could do some white knight stuff, because he had seen with his own eyes that Gene hadn't been very nice to her. He wondered how the man could have been so stupid as to leave her. JoLynne was pretty and funny, and it had been a long time since he had looked at a woman that way. Her long hair was dark gray with silver rivulets running through it, a little messy, like she didn't care that much. Nice body, too. She looked like she enjoyed a good meal and it didn't hurt her a bit. She wore a lot of rings, not on her ring finger, though.

He still couldn't imagine anybody forgiving Gene for what he did, dumping her for the secretary at the warehouse. Let alone taking care of him when he got sick. Seemed JoLynne and Beau had that in common, too—helping other people to the point of ridiculousness.

It would be nice if one day they could compare war stories, but she sure seemed gun-shy.

Buck snorted, tossing his head.

"Hang on, buddy. We'll get out of here in just a second."

Buck was a quarter horse gelding, the fiery one of the three. He had belonged to Beau's daughter, but Talia had to leave Buck behind when she moved into a condo in Studio City to work for an ad agency. The other riding horse, Shorty, was an oversized thoroughbred, a gentle mare Beau's son had saved from the rendering plant. Shorty was Beau's now, too, since Caleb had moved away as well.

And then there was Hashtag, a shaggy Shetland pony with the heart of a rodeo clown. He was always trying to steal things, like the rag Beau would hang out of his back pocket just for fun.

JoLynne would probably take to Buck, given her competition background.

Sitting next to her on the bench, watching her struggle with her feelings, it was like watching a documentary. Her face was so expressive, he could almost read each emotion flashing across the screen of her dark blue eyes. But then she would stifle them down.

She was tall, came up past his chin, and he was six feet. Used to be, anyway. Felt like he had shrunk a little. Everything changed after he turned fifty.

That was a big year, the year his wife served him with divorce papers.

"The kids are old enough to handle it now," she had said. Then she climbed into her boyfriend's sports car and drove away, leaving the three of them standing on the porch.

Talia, twelve at the time, had her arms wrapped tight around his waist, her face buried in his shirt. But Caleb, fifteen, had already turned and gone back in the house, slamming the door behind him.

For the next six years, until Talia left for college, Beau played mother and father both. Burning dinners, helping with math homework, trying to remember how to braid hair. And always wondering if he was failing.

He paused to snap a picture of the palomino in the slanting barn light and texted it to his daughter.

Your boy misses you.

Then he followed up.

Hey, your seaweed avocado shake powder's back at the co-op. Want me to grab some?

A second later, Talia sent a text with two thumbs-up emojis and a smiley face. It wasn't much, but she was a good girl, never left him hanging for long. He made a mental note to pick up the powder, happy to still have reason to be a dad with her. He tried not to hover, but parenting didn't shut off just because they moved out.

Nate's voice broke into his thoughts. "Thought I heard you out here."

"Work to do, if you're bored or anything," said Beau.

His younger brother stood framed in the barn doorway, his bald head reflecting the overhead light, his walrus mustache hiding his mouth, and his Levis hiding the titanium leg that replaced the one he had lost in the Gulf War.

"I'd give the horses some exercise." Beau shoved his phone into his back pocket. "Are you going to be hungry around five? I was planning to barbecue hamburgers."

"Yeah, whatever." Nate turned around and walked away, his limp only noticeable to Beau. After the war, he had returned to the ranch, helped their parents until their deaths, and then inherited all of it. But it was too much for him. Beau came home after the divorce, moved into the second house, and tried to keep the place from falling apart.

Alone in the silence of his brother's retreat, Beau worked the curry comb over Buck's hide in slow, practiced strokes. The gelding's golden coat had taken on a dusty sheen from the morning's roll in the paddock, and now the barn air filled with the scent of sun-warmed horse, hay, and the rich base note of leather. Dust motes drifted through the slats of sunlight slashing the aisle floor.

Buck shifted his weight, one hind leg cocked lazily.

"Don't get too comfortable, big shot," Beau muttered, pulling a burr from Buck's mane. "We're riding out in a minute."

Buck snorted in reply. The horse had always been dramatic, but he accepted grooming with noble resignation.

The barn was quiet except for the rustle of dry leaves and the soft thump of a moth against the window. From the next stall, Shorty gave her stall a little kick, just enough to remind Beau she was waiting her turn.

Beau glanced over. "You're next. Just be patient."

He slid a pad onto Buck's back, then hefted the saddle with a grunt. Buck sidestepped a little, testing him. Beau tightened the cinch, giving the strap a hard tug to check it, making sure it was snug.

He threw some grain to Shorty, gathered Buck's reins, and walked him out into the bright light of a southern California evening, the dust rising from the horse's hooves.

Outside, the warm air was rich with the scent of sage and chaparral rising off the nearby hills. Beau mounted up with a creak of leather, settling into the saddle like folding into an easy chair. Buck shied and gave a little kick, but Beau was ready for him. He gave him a gentle nudge with his heels, and they moved out at a relaxed walk.

He loved riding and wished he had more time for it, but he was just one man. Nate tended to stick close to the house, leaving most of the ranch work to Beau. There were fences to mend, horses to tend to, piping and woodwork to repair. Not to mention his job in town, a forty-minute commute.

He was tormented by signs of neglect around the ranch and wished he could do more, or maybe hire help, but Nate didn't want strangers poking into their business.

The trail to the creek was narrow and winding, bordered by a low rail fence on one side and scrub on the other. Dry grass brushed Beau's work boots, and occasional branches reached out trying to snag him. The horse's hooves clopped rhythmically on the hard-packed earth, and Beau let the motion lull his thoughts, his hand resting loosely on the saddle horn.

He thought JoLynne would enjoy riding the little quarter horse.

"Get your head out of the clouds," he said to himself. "She's never coming here."

Buck tossed his head, and Beau gave him a pat. "She'd like you, buddy. You're both tough."

He wondered where a person got that kind of confidence. JoLynne didn't seem broken at all. She looked calm and controlled. Until she opened the bag and saw the picture. Then she fell apart and ran off.

Beau winced. He hadn't meant to hurt her. Maybe he should give her a call, see if there was any apologizing due.

Sure, buddy, he told himself. It has nothing to do with you wanting to see her again. Beau didn't have time for a relationship, busy as he was. Sometimes, the thought bothered him. He was almost at retirement age. Maybe he ought to start thinking about what came next.

Nah.

He flicked the reins and kept on going.

Three

JoLynne adjusted the collar of her blazer with nervous precision. She stepped back from the mirror, turned sideways, and gave herself the once-over. "Still got it," she murmured, though the words came out more like a question than a declaration.

The morning sunlight through the bedroom curtains lit the room with an optimistic glow. She ran a hand over her iron-gray hair, tucking behind her ears the silver strands that sprang from her temples. Lastly, she added a touch of lipstick, a nice shade, one of the expensive ones she had kept from her office days. "You ran that office like a well-oiled machine," she told her reflection. "You trained half the people who came through there, including Frank. You caught the shit before it hit the fan and guided the office to prosperity. They need you now, even if they do not know it yet."

They would be idiots not to hire you back. Her sister's voice echoed in her head. JoLynne smiled, wide and rehearsed, then held it for three seconds like Vivian had told her.

"Stand tall," Vivian had said. "You're professional, but casual. You're not begging. You've got something to sell if they're smart enough to buy it."

JoLynne picked up her red shoulder bag, the one that still smelled faintly of leather and breath mints, and grabbed her car keys.

At the office in downtown Serena Cove, the glass door hissed shut behind her, and for a second JoLynne just stood there, blinking against the slick whiteness of the new paint. A clean, minimalist sign on the wall read:

SOUTHCOAST INSURANCE GROUP

Protecting What Matters Most

JoLynne took a slow step forward. The old burgundy carpet was gone, replaced by a charcoal-gray laminate that looked like wood if you squinted. The walls had been redone in a greige linen wallpaper, and the front desk was new and blazing white, with a mounted touchscreen kiosk on one side. She half expected someone to ask for her coffee order.

Behind the desk sat a woman in her early twenties. She looked up with an overly bright smile. "Hi there! Can I help you?"

JoLynne approached the desk. "I'm here to see Frank Mumford. I used to work for him and wanted to say hi."

"Oh, cool!" the girl chirped, already typing something. "And what's your name?"

"JoLynne Malloy. I mean, Coltrane. It's Coltrane now." In her nervousness, she forgot she had reverted to her maiden name after the divorce.

The receptionist's eyebrows flicked up, almost imperceptibly, like the name rang a very faint bell. She glanced down at her screen again. "Okay, awesome, I'll let him know you're here."

JoLynne took a slow look around the waiting area. There were more chairs now, sleeker ones in gray vinyl instead of the padded navy ones she had special-ordered twelve years ago because they were firm enough for older clients. She scanned the wall where the local high school team photos used to hang, but they were gone, replaced by brushed metal frames with smiling stock-photo families, everyone annoyingly symmetrical and white-toothed.

Two customers sat waiting, one of them glaring at his watch, the other flipping through a laminated flyer. The phones rang steadily. She heard one line go to voicemail. Then another. JoLynne folded her arms. This place needed her.

The receptionist returned, again flashing the enhanced smile. "He'll be right with you. Why don't you have a seat?"

But before she could do so, a familiar voice rang out. "Is that JoLynne?"

It was Zane, one of the junior agents she had trained five years ago. He was older now, maybe thirty, and wearing a slightly too tight sport coat over a prosperous paunch.

"Wow, long time no see!" he said, walking over with a laugh, holding out his hand. "What are you doing here?"

JoLynne gave him a confident smile. "Hoping to come back."

Zane's face froze for a fleeting second. "Oh. Uh huh. That's great."

"You don't sound all that thrilled."

The man laughed nervously. "I mean, I would be. It's just that I think we're pretty full up right now. Like staff-wise. And there've been a lot of changes since you left. We've completely upgraded our system."

She nodded slowly. "I like new systems, if you remember."

Behind them, another phone rang. No one picked it up. Zane glanced at the waiting clients, flashing them an over-amped smile.

Then a booming voice reached her from the hallway.

"JoLynne Malloy, as I live and breathe! Get on over here!"

Her smile was genuine as she turned, and then she had to work to keep it because the shock was profound. Frank Mumford had changed. He was leaner now, almost wiry. His jaw was more angular without the soft fold of his former double chin. He had shaved his thinning hair down to a clean buzz cut, which somehow made his cheekbones look faintly cadaverous. He wore a tailored button-down with sleeves rolled to the elbow, showing off forearms that had clearly seen the inside of a gym. It was like looking at a human piece of beef jerky.

"Frank," she said, holding out her hand to shake.

He strode over, arms wide, enveloping her in a hug that lasted one beat too long, as if trying to project warmth he did not quite feel. Then he pulled back, his smile calculating.

"Damn, it's good to see you," he said. "You look great."

"So do you," she replied.

Niceties out of the way, he held out his hand in a courtly gesture. "Come on back," he said. "Let's catch up."

She followed him past the bullpen, past three desks that hadn't existed when she left, past an intern with a septum ring who was taking a personal call in what used to be the fax room. Frank's new office had been redone too. It was bigger now, with glass walls and a faux-wood desk that looked like something off a design blog. There was a whiteboard covered in color-coded tasks, a standing desk contraption, and a sleek monitor arm holding twin screens. A logo water bottle sat by his mousepad.

He motioned for her to sit, then propped his rear end on the edge of his desk.

"I was sorry to hear about Gene," he said, brow furrowed. "How've you been holding up?"

She smiled, calm. "Really good, thanks. I'm glad I could help him."

Frank shook his head. "You're a saint, JoLynne."

"I did what anybody would do," she said. "And now I'm ready to get back to work. In fact, that's why I'm here, because I'm wondering if you have a spot for me. Even part time, if that would be helpful. I know the ropes, and you've got twice the staff now, which means twice the clutter if you're not careful."

"Boy, that is the truth. You know how it goes." Frank sighed and glanced toward his window. Outside, the parking lot was bustling, and beyond that, traffic started and stopped on the highway. The town was getting busier with each passing year. No doubt, so was the office.

"It looks like business is good," she said.

"That's a pretty decent assessment." He crossed his legs, knitting his hands over one knee. "It's true that we're really busy, but with technology, it's easy to get a lot more done with less. So we're in real good shape."

"I believe you," she said with manufactured enthusiasm. "It's a new day. Greater efficiency and productivity. I've kept up."

His eyes shifted to the side. "Thing is, Jo, we've modernized a lot since you were here. More automation. Cross-departmental systems. Most of our filing is cloud-based. We've got new integrations, new everything. It's a whole new world."

JoLynne raised an eyebrow. "So, fewer mistakes?"

"Let's just say they're different these days." Frank laughed.

"I can adapt."

"No doubt," he said quickly. "It's just, we've got a younger team now. A lot of them came in already trained on these platforms. You'd be looking at a steep tech curve."

He winced even as he said it. She saw the flush rise under his collar. There was a long silence.

"Look, Jo." He leaned forward, "I was always impressed by your work ethic, your brains. Christ, you could outthink anybody on the floor. But things are different now. Anyway, you don't want to be inside, slaving over a hot desk. Go have fun, have lunch with your friends, see a movie. You've earned a break."

"What if I don't want a break, Frank? I'm ready to be back in action, making things run better for the office. You know I'm capable. I can help."

The receptionist tapped on the glass. "Your eleven o'clock is here, Frank."

Frank looked down at his nails. They were buffed and shiny. "Well, Jo, like I said, we're fully staffed right now. But if something comes up, you'll be the first call I make." He held out his hand.

JoLynne stood up, her smile brittle. "Thank you for your time."

He paused at his office door, adding, "And hey, really good seeing you."

"You too, Frank."

No one looked up as she slipped out the door. Outside, the sun beat down mercilessly and the parking lot shimmered with heat. She stood for a moment by her car, holding her keys, letting it all settle. Recalling the slick decor, the fake smiles, and the cold politeness of a place she used to run like a tight ship, her stomach rolled. Sick with humiliation, she unlocked her car and slid behind the wheel. Inside, the air was stale and hot. She turned the ignition, rolled down the windows, got back out, peeled off her blazer and tossed it in the back seat, got back in, and slammed the door. "'You'll be the first call I make,'" she growled. "What a jackass."

Gripping the wheel, she pulled out of the parking lot maybe a little too quickly, sunglasses on, mouth set. The sky above Serena Cove was irritatingly blue with puffball clouds, and all around her, smiling tourists strolled the sidewalks. Waiting for a gaggle of middle-aged shoppers to cross in front of her car, JoLynne clenched and unclenched her jaw, reliving the last wasted half-hour of her life.

"'Steep tech curve'"? Was he serious? Frank, who used to rely on her to explain his own emails to him? She had implemented new systems that were probably still running the place.

The traffic slowed as she wound her way through downtown Serena Cove, and her heart ached. She had loved working in the village. Now, it felt like she was done. Old, retired, washed-up.

She slammed on the brakes as a car darted out of a side street, oblivious. "Asshole," she muttered, waiting for the car to get out of her way, thinking about how it seemed she was always in reaction mode, and she was sick of it.

This is not how the rest of her life was supposed to go.

"I am not a victim," she pronounced loudly to the empty car. "I will find something. I am going to be happy, and I am going to have a great life if it kills me."

By the end of the sentence, she was practically yelling. And then a message came into her mind, spoken in Vivian's laughing voice.

The jackass was right. You're free now. This is your time. Live bigger.

JoLynne blinked, the wheel steady in her hands. That's when the idea struck. Sudden and dumb and delicious.

Beau.

She hadn't talked to him since the day he gave her the photo. He had tried to be kind, but she had practically galloped away from him, needing to escape because beyond the shock of the photo, it was the sense that he cared how she handled it, standing ready to offer his support. His kindness had overwhelmed her, and when you coupled that with his good looks and that rich, deep voice, well, the attraction was just too shocking, too strong.

And it had been mutual. A woman could tell.

JoLynne got a little shiver of excitement at the realization that she could march right into his workplace without notice. She could apologize for her abruptness and then see if he might want to meet for a drink or coffee or something. Might as well. She was all dressed up.

But it had been a while since she'd flirted with a man, and she was out of practice. Maybe this was a dumb idea.

Her refrigerator list said otherwise.

Be brave, she told herself. What was the worst that could happen? *He's not interested, you're embarrassed, you walk away and never see him again. You'll live.*

Remembering the route to Gene's old office, she turned off the highway.

Hot damn. She was really doing this.

Her smile was so big it almost hurt.

Four

The late afternoon wind coming in off the ocean cut through JoLynne's sweatshirt as she steered her golf cart toward Ursula's house. Even in July, Serena Cove afternoons could be freezing, and gray clouds were clumping together and beginning to block out the sky.

Cass had texted two days ago:

Ursula's firepit, Wed 4:30. First meeting of the Serena Cove Social Committee. Be there!

And because of the list staring at her from her refrigerator, JoLynne had RSVP'd that she'd be there.

That list was getting her into all kinds of good trouble.

When she'd surprised Beau at work, he was delighted. He told his assistant to handle his calls and took JoLynne on a tour. Introduced her to everyone, making sure she had a minute to update people who still remembered Gene, and gave her the lowdown on the work they were doing.

And then there was the moment he'd grabbed her with both hands on her arms and quickly moved her out of the way of a forklift that came hurrying past. Her skin had buzzed with his touch, and he didn't let go right away.

So there was that.

But also, it was fun to see him in that environment. The enjoyment of his job shone in his eyes. He commanded the warehouse floor, now laughing, now directing, stopping every five feet to answer someone's question or jot something down on his phone. Although she did notice he wore that slightly frazzled look of a person in charge of too many things.

Now, as she stepped around the corner of the house, the scent of wood smoke hit her nostrils, earthy and rich. There was a hum of voices, and a sharp burst of laughter. JoLynne hesitated, but then took a breath and plowed forward.

In the backyard, the members of the book club as well as some new people were seated on mismatched lawn chairs circling the stone firepit, paper plates balanced on knees, red SOLO cups in hand. It seemed everyone was talking at once.

The yard was half wild with succulents and sea lavender going crazy in Ursula's rock garden and a tiki torch listing sideways. A folding table held cookies, snacks, and coffee. A bottle of brandy stood nearby, and a couple of people were waiting to add it to their coffee mugs.

JoLynne spotted Cass near the snack table and made her way over, her tennies already wet from the damp grass.

"There's decaf," Cass said by way of greeting, waving a spoon toward the carafes. "Vanilla, chocolate, or cinnamon."

"I brought wine, but I think I'll donate it." JoLynne reached for the brandy. They stood together for a moment, shoulder to shoulder, Cass in her signature quilted vest, JoLynne in sweats and a knit scarf.

"It's a good turnout, don't you think?" asked Cass.

"Yeah. Do you know all these people?"

Cass scanned the group. "Not yet."

Just then, Dan and Teresa arrived, Dan hauling a bundle of firewood under one arm. Ursula, in full black from her ankle boots to her ski sweater, directed him where to put it. Dan obeyed and then joined Teresa at the snack table, bumping his hip against hers. She turned and melted into his side like a smitten teenager.

JoLynne and Cass grabbed a pair of canvas chairs near the fire and settled in, the orange glow flickering across their faces. Whatever this was, it wasn't a party, but it didn't feel like anything official. JoLynne's curiosity grew. She hoped she didn't regret coming out on this chilly afternoon.

After a moment, Cass stood up, clutching her travel mug in one hand and signaling with the other to call for quiet. "Everybody, can I get your attention?"

The conversation around the firepit quieted, people turning toward her with curiosity and politeness.

JoLynne raised her mug and took a sip, waiting.

Cass looked around the circle. "First, I want to thank Ursula for letting us meet here. I had hoped we could gather on the beach, but we would have frozen to death."

Ursula gave her a regal nod. "You are welcome."

"So, here's the thing." Cass took a deep breath. "Some of you knew my mom. She lived here for years, and she loved it. My dad, too. One of the things Mom always said was how much she missed the old days. When they used to have community events here in the park. Barbecues, game nights, pool parties. I particularly remember her talking about an annual cardboard boat race?"

One old woman called out, "I still have sunburn from that day." Several people laughed, nodding.

"Anyway," Cass said, "ever since we started the book club, I've had people ask me: could we do more? Could we have more social stuff? You know, simple, fun activities that get people out of their houses and talking to each other again. So I'm asking you if you think that might be a good idea, and if so, what might we do?"

A few people murmured in agreement.

Cass pressed on. "I know we're not all looking for the same thing. Some of us would rather stay in our homes, locked up tight. A bunch of us are still working. Some of us are caring for partners, or grieving, or just figuring things out. And that can be really lonely."

JoLynne felt something shift in her chest. She looked away, down toward the roiling gray waters of the ocean.

Cass continued, "What do you think? What if we tried a few little things? A movie night. A game night. Maybe another pool party."

"The last one was so much fun, you got engaged again," shouted Kellie, the dog groomer.

"That's right! I did." Cass wiggled her left hand in the air, smiling and showing off her ring.

Teresa stood up. "I suggest we don't make it real formal. Let's just find out what people want. Let it grow organically, like the book club did."

"Good idea," said Cass.

There was a long pause. Then Ursula said, "I suggest a night with wine and board games. Residents could bring whatever games they wanted and teach others how to play. In this way, those who joined in would not be alone."

JoLynne blinked. It was the longest speech she'd heard Ursula make. In the firepit, a log snapped in half, sending a shower of sparks skyward.

Bernie, Cass's elderly neighbor, raised his hand. "I vote we have movies. Especially if they're loud and nobody talks through them."

"Could do bingo," someone called out. "I've got the cards."

JoLynne sat back, watching it all unfold, a smile tugging at her lips. Cass was a real organizer, and ever since she'd decided to stay, the park had a new energy. The discussion took on steam. As the conversation became more animated, Cass slipped back in her chair next to JoLynne.

"Are you done stirring things up?" JoLynne asked.

"They don't need me," said Cass. "I can relax and let them hash it out." She went to the snack table, splashed a bit more brandy in both their cups, and sat back down. She and JoLynne tapped coffee cups.

"So now, tell me," said Cass. "Whatever happened with that guy who came looking for you at the clubhouse a couple days ago?"

JoLynne's face grew hot. She tilted her head down into her coffee, hiding a smile. "We went to the bench and talked for a while," she said. "Beau used to work with Gene, and he found something at the job that got left behind. He thought I'd want it. That's all."

"He was pretty good-looking for an old guy." Cass covered her mouth. "Oh, sorry! That was bad."

"That *was* bad, youngster."

"Had you ever met him before, when you were married?"

"I think so. I really don't remember." JoLynne looked away so her young friend couldn't read the lie in her eyes. Of course, she remembered Beau. How could anyone not? In the years of seeing him at company picnics, she'd noticed how different he was from the other men Gene worked with. He was smart-mouthed and funny, and got along with everybody. Truly a good guy.

Today, she'd been able to apologize. And then some.

Cass elbowed her gently. "So, are you going to see him again?"

JoLynne couldn't help it. She smiled.

"You are!" Cass held up her palm for a high-five. "Way to get back out there, girl."

Beau had been more than gracious, even offering to take her to lunch, but when his assistant popped out and reminded him of a meeting, he had winced, genuinely disappointed.

"Rain check?" he asked, his mouth quirking up. "How about we go riding at my place on Saturday? I've got a horse that'd be perfect for you."

Gathering her courage, JoLynne had agreed. And then they'd said good-bye, beaming at each other, and she'd walked out of that warehouse, her feet barely hitting the ground.

"Look at you, trying something new," she had chortled, speeding along the highway with the windows down. Screw that insurance office. JoLynne had taken a chance and had a fabulous afternoon.

Because touring the warehouse with him, feeling the brush of his hand on her lower back as she preceded him through a doorway, the little thrill of a man's touch...

She had laughed at herself in the rearview mirror. *Oh, girl, you are in trouble already.*

"What about you?" she asked Cass. "Where's that cute new husband of yours?"

Cass shrugged. "He's on the road all week."

"I thought he was giving up that job for something local."

"He is, but his boss asked him to hang around another month. It's their busy time. But on the bright side, I have time to work on my business. I landed two new clients in town. They want to replace their data systems, and I'm helping."

"Congratulations," said JoLynne. "That's what you wanted, right?"

"It is," Cass nodded happily, but then got pulled away by the discussion.

Someone asked if they could use the clubhouse for bingo nights. Some-one else grumbled about Diane's calendar system, which led to Diane loudly explaining the calendar system, which led to Ursula offering to redesign it in Excel, which led to Dan murmuring something about how God Himself didn't understand Excel.

Chuck, the handyman, cleared his throat. "I have an idea," he said. Chuck didn't speak that often, and the group fell silent. He stared at the grass in front of him for a second before continuing. "I've been looking at the lighting situation around the pool deck."

"Yes, that's all finished, and we appreciate your efforts," Diane said, clearly ready to move on.

"It's not ideal after dusk, is my thought," said Chuck. "It might be worth installing a few low-voltage LEDs along the perimeter. It'd be safer and would let people use the hot tub after dinner without fumbling around in the dark."

Diane rolled her eyes. "We don't let people use the hot tub after dark."

Chuck nodded once, brushed his mustache with a finger, and locked eyes with Diane. "We could, though, is what I'm saying."

She looked at him then, assessing. He held her gaze.

Diane's eyebrows rose slightly. Then she looked down at her papers. "I'll bring it to the board."

Chuck gave a tiny smile, gone as fast as it appeared. JoLynne elbowed Cass, who snorted softly.

The fire burned down and the sky grew dark, but no one seemed in a rush to leave. That was the real surprise. No one was checking their phone. No one was reaching for their keys. They just lingered. Talking, warming their hands, tossing around good ideas and bad ones.

But eventually, folks started to stand, stretch, and fold up their chairs. JoLynne stood too, brushing cookie crumbs off her lap. She had half a mind to slip away quietly. To let herself be carried home on the high of having shown up and participated.

But it was enough for one day. Maybe even a week.

Diane appeared at her elbow like a tactically deployed drone.

"So," she said.

JoLynne groaned. "Oh no. What now?"

"We need a treasurer."

"I told you, I do bookkeeping. I'm not a treasurer."

"You were, before Gene made you quit."

"He didn't make me do anything. I got tired of being on the board, is all."

Diane collected the remaining coffee mugs and paper towels. "Well, I need you to come back. And in return, the HOA will rehire you in your old job."

JoLynne stared at her, suspicious. "How much?"

"State minimum, the same as before," Diane said.

First, a social committee, then working in the office, then her old board position back. If she didn't look out, JoLynne would never have a quiet moment to herself.

Cass cut in gently. "You should take it. Nobody else knows the job like you."

JoLynne made a disrespectful sound. Cass was just being nice because it wasn't that much of a job, but JoLynne needed to cobble together something before she was really strapped for money.

She folded her arms. Diane fussed with a stack of napkins, waiting for an answer.

"Okay, fine. If you're going to extort me like that, I guess I'll have to be your bookkeeper."

"Treasurer." Diane nodded. "Good. The first meeting of the full board is next week. I'll send you an email."

"Full? Who else did you get?"

"You, me, and Cass," said Diane. "And Chuck might want to sit in." Her stony visage had softened. "He seems to think he can play some kind of role."

JoLynne looked closer. If she wasn't mistaken, Diane was blushing.

The crowd was thinning out as the flames settled into embers. Dan offered to douse the fire, but Ursula, who kept glancing to the east, told him not to bother, that she would be outside for a while yet.

Cass and JoLynne cleared the folding table and headed for the back door of the house.

"That was a good meeting, don't you think?" Cass set a load of dirty cups on the sink. "It was good to see you mingling."

JoLynne loaded the dishwasher. "I'm just adjusting. It's been a while since I had this many conversations in one day."

"You're rusty," said Cass. "But this is good for you. It'll get easier."

"I guess," said JoLynne. This was what she wanted, wasn't it? After three years of virtual isolation, with the stress and loneliness and everyday grinding down of caregiving for a man she didn't even like that much, reentry into the world of the park was turning out to be head-spinning.

So now she had a job, however minor. A board position. Friends circling around her like she was part of something again. And a man waiting for her at the end of the week. A man who was intrigued by her, who seemed to get her, even if he didn't know the whole of her yet.

She caught herself smiling.

"Something funny?" Cass asked.

JoLynne shook her head. "Just happy. I think."

"Be careful. You don't want to get ahead of yourself."

JoLynne laughed and bumped knuckles with her young friend. They walked back toward their carts, the evening wind picking up again, but JoLynne didn't mind the cold anymore. Her hair was windblown, cheeks pink from the fire, a smile still lingering on her face.

"Look at you, gettin' all social," she said, grinning into the wind as the cart sped toward home.

Five

JoLynne arrived at Beau's ranch late Saturday morning, feeling a flutter of nerves. She wore her old boots, jeans that still fit, and a sensible hat that served more as a sun shield than a fashion statement. She spotted a horse trailer where Beau stood near two other people, a man and a woman. He looked up when he noticed her arrival and strode over eagerly as she parked. He opened her car door and remarked favorably on her boots, which were fawn colored with pink and turquoise inlays.

"I won them years ago. They still fit," she said.

"They look great," he replied. "You'll be on Buck."

"Is he named that because of his behavior?"

Beau laughed. "No, he's a good horse." He eyed the nylon fanny pack in her hand. "You're welcome to stash that in my saddlebag, if you'd rather not wear it."

JoLynne, suddenly self-conscious, said, "I might have brought too much."

"It'll fit," he said. "And I've got plenty of water, too. So, all you need to do is enjoy the ride."

They walked over to the trailer where the other couple was tacking up their two horses. The man was short and lean, with a gray beard and a ball cap from an old rodeo. The woman beside him wore sunglasses and a long blonde braid, and was tugging at her horse's girth strap.

"JoLynne, this is Mike and Tanya. They live a couple miles from here."

Mike's handshake was firm and warm, and Tanya flashed a welcoming smile.

"Glad you came out. It's a beautiful day for a ride."

"Good to meet you. I'm pretty excited," said JoLynne, still adjusting to the rhythm of this place, this easy warmth. "It's been a while."

"You'll do fine," said Beau. "Let's go meet your horse."

A pony whinnied from inside the barn.

"You have another one in there?" she asked.

"That's Hashtag," Beau said. "He's not coming with us, and he's bummed out about it. I'll introduce you later."

Beyond the low fence, two horses stood already saddled and tied at the rail, flicking their tails lazily. The smaller one, a stocky golden palomino with a white blaze, lifted his head at the sound of footsteps.

"This one's yours," Beau said. "Say hi to Buck."

JoLynne stepped up, hand outstretched. "Hey, handsome," she murmured, her voice soft and low. "You remember how this works?" Holding her hand just under his nose, she let him sniff. His ears twitched forward, and he blew on her hand, getting a read on her. She patted his neck, picked up the reins, and swung a leg over. She settled into the saddle like it hadn't been decades. It felt so right, her eyes stung. How long had it been? Forty years if a day.

"How're the stirrups?" Beau asked, standing by her side.

She wiggled her boots in the iron. "Perfect."

"Okay then." Grabbing the saddle horn of the sleek bay, Beau thrust his boot into the stirrup and swung aboard, the leather creaking under him, and JoLynne couldn't help but notice the way his Levi's curved perfectly over a nicely shaped behind. Nothing like a good-looking cowboy. She bit back a smile.

They wheeled their horses around toward Mike and Tanya, who were already mounted and waiting at the trailhead.

The little group moved out at a walk. Hooves thudded gently against the packed dirt as they passed the paddocks and left the ranch behind, winding through oak and eucalyptus groves on sun-dappled trails. The air smelled of dust and wild fennel. The other couple moved out front, giving Beau and JoLynne space to talk privately.

"Is this all yours?" she asked, gesturing at the surrounding acreage. On either side of the trail, dry hills rolled gently upward, dotted with granite outcroppings and the occasional coyote bush. The sun was warm but not punishing, the sky cloudless above. A red-tailed hawk circled overhead, tracing wide arcs over the hills.

Beau nodded. "I grew up here. The ranch has been in my family for three generations now." There was no swagger to his words, just quiet pride.

"So this is your backyard. Not bad."

He smiled, eyes shaded by the brim of his Stetson. "For a kid, it was paradise. You'll see when we get to the creek. Feels like a whole different world down there."

Mike and Tanya disappeared around a bend, followed by the soft clop of hooves on a wooden bridge. The trail narrowed slightly, dipping into a shallow ravine where cottonwoods leaned overhead, their leaves whispering in the breeze.

"Careful in here," Beau said. "It'll get steeper along the trail down to the creek, and the footing changes."

Buck's ears twitched forward as the scent of water reached them. They descended into the gulch, where shadows pooled under the canopy and the air turned earthy and sweet. Tall sycamores arched over the trail, their pale trunks peeling like old parchment, and thick grass grew in patches beneath the trees. Somewhere nearby, a creek murmured, half-hidden under a tangle of willow and reeds.

JoLynne breathed it in. The hush, the green, the light filtering down like lace through the leaves—it felt almost holy. Ahead of her, Beau was quiet, eyes scanning the trail, hand easy on the reins. He belonged here, and yet the way he held his shoulders hinted at a weight carried behind all that ease.

Buck picked his way confidently over a patch of exposed stone, and JoLynne reached down to pat his neck.

"You ride like you never quit," said Beau.

"It feels good to be on a horse," she said. "I can't thank you enough for inviting me."

He smiled at her, his eyes crinkling at the corners. "Glad you're here." He clicked his tongue and his horse moved off.

JoLynne followed behind, admiring his broad shoulders and the easy sway of his spine as his horse walked ahead. They rode in silence for a while, the horses splashing as they crossed the creek once and then again. The air smelled of mud and wet vegetation. A blue dragonfly buzzed past JoLynne's knee. She inhaled deeply, letting it all sink in.

With the creak of the saddle, the clomp of the horses' hooves occasionally ringing off a rock, and the jingle of their bridles, she felt peace settle over her. If she closed her eyes, she was back in Montana, back on the ranch riding with her dad and the hands, rounding up cows and calves in the springtime, looking forward to a filling lunch of stew and biscuits. A couple of cups of coffee and they'd mount up again, finishing out the day exhausted but happy, knowing the ranch's future was assured.

As his horse walked on, Beau turned to catch her daydreaming.

"You good?"

"I'm great," she said, beaming.

He pushed his hat up with his thumb and nodded before riding on. Watching him now, ahead of her, relaxed in the saddle, she felt as if they shared a history, as if they had a life in common from some place long ago, back in time, in her imagination.

Eventually, Mike called a halt, and they dismounted in a shady spot right next to the creek. The four of them tied their horses in such a way as to let them graze.

"Great spot," said JoLynne, finding a seat on the fallen log that faced the creek.

"I've always enjoyed stopping here," said Tanya. "We take breaks, have a little snack, let the horses rest."

"The tree makes such a perfect seat, it's like it fell here on purpose," said JoLynne.

"That was our goal." Beau cracked open a bottle of water and handed it to her. "Few years ago, there was a big storm. A real gully washer."

"I remember that," said Tanya.

"A few days later, after the water went back down, my brother and I came down here with a couple of guys to get the tree out of the creek because it was damming it up. It took all day, but we sawed off limbs and dragged it around to where it'd be like a bench."

"You did a good job," said Mike.

"Where's your brother now?" asked JoLynne.

Beau took a long draught of water, his throat moving as he swallowed. Then he capped the bottle and held it loosely in one hand. "I would imagine he's home," he said, avoiding her eyes.

JoLynne decided that if she wanted to know more, she might have to wait.

"How's your new horse working out?" Beau asked Tanya, with a nod toward the chestnut mare.

"She's a doll," Tanya said, beaming. She set off on a story about rescuing the mare from a neglectful owner, nursing her back to health, and discovering just how smart and good-natured the horse was. It turned out Tanya was a veterinarian. She and Beau had met when he brought in a pet dog who was old and suffering, and Dr. Tanya had helped him ease the dog along on his celestial journey.

JoLynne could see that the memory still hurt, which only made her like him more. She shook her head as if trying to clear it, to resist, because there was a lot to like about Beau Landry. He was kind, good-looking, and he took good care of his animals. The ranch looked well-tended, although there were some spots that needed attention. A tree had died next to the house, for example, and it should be taken down and hauled off to reduce the risk of fire. And there was a broken-down car in the yard, covered with a faded canvas tarp.

"Is Nate doing better?" Tanya asked softly.

"He's fine," said Beau. He looked at JoLynne. "My brother lives here. Up at the main house."

"You two live together?"

"There's another house on the property," he said. "That one's mine."

She waited for more, but when he fell silent, she followed suit, turning back to the creek to watch a couple of sparrows dipping and bathing on the other side.

"I hate to say it, but we should probably get back," said Tanya. "I'm on staff this evening."

"No way," said Beau. "I've got four steaks marinating."

Mike groaned, but Tanya stood up. "How fast can you cook them?"

They mounted up and rode single file back along the creek, up the slope and out of the gulch, and back toward the ranch, this time with more urgency. Once again on the flats, Beau rode alongside JoLynne.

"It's nice of you to cook for us," she said.

"You haven't eaten yet," said Beau. "I burn things a lot."

She laughed.

They talked about his work at the warehouse, and she described life at the park, how she was just starting to branch out a little, making friends now that she was free of caregiving.

"Yeah, that's healthy," he said. "You went through a lot. With Gene, I mean. Taking care of him all that time."

She shook her head. It was too nice a day to dwell on the negatives.

Back at the ranch, the sun was dipping low. Hashtag, the pony, too small to ride but full of personality, greeted them at the fence, demanding attention. He nosed JoLynne's boots and tried to nip her foot. She laughed.

After unsaddling the horses and turning them out, the four of them walked up a driveway behind the main house, which led to the back side of a smaller home.

"This is mine," Beau said, swinging open a patio gate.

"What a pretty yard," said JoLynne.

"I think so, too," said Tanya.

"He's got a real sense of garden design," said Mike.

"You're just jealous," said Beau. "Let's rustle up some grub and we'll get you on your way."

He fired up the gas grill while Tanya microwaved baked potatoes and JoLynne started pouring four glasses of red wine.

"Not for me," said Tanya. "I have to work."

Mike threw together a salad, looking like he was comfortable in Beau's kitchen, while Tanya found silverware and condiments for the table on the patio. When the steaks were ready, Beau piled them on a platter, and everybody loaded up their plates and carried them outside. They fell into easy conversation, talking about horses and kids and jobs.

Dinner was enjoyable, but a little rushed. When they were carrying their empty plates inside, JoLynne joined Tanya rinsing dishes at the sink.

Tanya lowered her voice and said, "It's good to see Beau having fun."

"Doesn't he usually?" asked JoLynne.

"He's stretched awful thin, with his job and commuting and the ranch to take care of."

"But his brother lives here," said JoLynne.

"Nate's not a lot of help."

They quickly changed the subject when Beau came in from the patio, his face easy, unaware of the shift in tone. Tanya dried her hands on a dish towel and smiled at Mike.

"We should hit the road," she said. "I need to clean up before going to work."

Mike stood, stretched his back, and went to fetch their things. Tanya gave JoLynne a warm squeeze on the arm. "I hope we see you again."

"Me too," JoLynne replied, meaning it.

There were hugs, promises to ride again soon, and a few good-natured parting jokes. The screen door creaked open, then slapped shut behind them, leaving JoLynne and Beau alone on the porch, the last hum of voices trailing down the driveway.

"You don't have to leave yet, do you?" he asked. The look in his eyes was welcoming, no pressure. But she could see the hopefulness, too.

"Let's sit on the swing," she said.

The silence that followed was gentle, not awkward, just two people suddenly aware of the quiet. She had not expected to feel this comfortable here. She hadn't expected to feel much of anything, but now the air between them felt charged.

Beau leaned back in the swing, one arm stretched along the back behind her shoulders, watching her with a softness in his expression that made her pulse tick faster.

"I'm glad you came today."

"Me too."

"Can I get you a drink? I've got some nice late-harvest Zinfandel that's amazing."

She pushed the swing, moving back and forth for a minute. "I should probably switch to water. It wouldn't be great if I got pulled over."

Beau reached for her hand and held it on his thigh, rocking with her. "You don't have to go," he said. His voice was low and easy. It was just a suggestion.

She did not answer right away. She looked out toward the darkened yard, where the last streaks of orange had faded from the sky. Her car keys sat on the counter inside. She could go and get them. Pound a tall glass of water and hit the road.

JoLynne glanced at him. Her voice was quiet. "I wasn't planning to stay."

"I know," he said. "I wasn't thinking that way either, until you came to the warehouse." He picked up her hand and held it against his mouth, his breath warm against her skin. "And then every minute since."

She sat quietly for a moment longer, heart thudding. She should go. That had been the plan—get in her car, drive back to her little house, slip into her routine like nothing had shifted.

But something had shifted.

It wasn't about being lonely. She wanted him for his warmth, for the way they fit together. But there was something else she couldn't quite put her finger on. It was like a bone-deep recognition of someone who knew what you knew.

It had tugged at something old in her, something familiar.

She looked at him now, easy and open, no pressure in his eyes, just that same steady presence that had made her say yes to coming out here in the first place.

Maybe she didn't need to play it safe. Not tonight.

Her fingers curled slightly in his hand. "How good is the Zin?"

He tilted his head back in a soundless laugh. "Very, very good."

JoLynne nodded. Then she leaned closer, tucking herself against his side. "Okay," she said. "I'll stay."

Six

B eau was pouring himself a cup of coffee when JoLynne came down
the hall. Hearing her footsteps, he turned, and his breath hitched.
Barefoot and smiling, she looked beautiful in his burgundy robe, her hair
adorably messy around her shoulders.

"Hey, you," he said, coming over to her and taking her by the elbows. He
drew her close and kissed her, then held her against his chest. Last night
was amazing. He still couldn't believe she'd chosen to stay. He tilted her
chin up to meet his eyes. "You ready for coffee?"

"I'd kill for a cup," she said, looking up at him, her voice raspy with sleep.

He forced himself to release her and went to fill her coffee mug.

"Have a seat." He opened the oven door and, using a dish towel, withdrew a hot baking pan. "I made blueberry muffins."

She tilted her head. "How long have you been up?"

"A while," he said. "The horses like an early breakfast." He poured their
coffee and slid a plate of warm muffins her way.

Taking a bite, she closed her eyes. "This is amazing."

"I try," he said modestly.

His phone buzzed on the counter, and he reached over to grab it. "It's my son, Caleb."

JoLynne raised an eyebrow. "He's up early, too."

"Yeah. I'd asked if he wanted to go see the Padres. They're at home." Beau looked at her. "Are you into baseball?"

She put up both hands as if warding him off.

Smiling, he tapped out a quick reply and set the phone down.

"So, are you two going?"

"Only if I let him buy all the food and drinks." He dipped his head. "I tend to hover."

JoLynne sipped her coffee. "Sounds like you're a good dad."

"I tried. The three of us, after the divorce, we stuck pretty close. Like a little pirate crew. Everyone got a scar, but we made it."

They were sitting down, cutting into the muffins, when someone knocked on the front door. Beau stiffened. There was nobody else who would arrive this early. He braced himself and went to see.

Nate stood on the porch, holding a tray of cinnamon rolls. As usual, his shirt was rumpled, and his denim shorts revealed a titanium prosthesis. "Saw you had company. Thought you could use these."

The two brothers looked at each other, tension between them. Classic Nate, barging into Beau's business. "Thanks, I guess."

Nate glanced around. "You going to invite me in?"

"I'm not sure that's—"

Beau stopped, feeling JoLynne behind him at the door.

"Is this your brother?" She reached around Beau, grinning. "Hi. I'm JoLynne."

"Nate," he said with a friendly nod.

Beau sighed. "Don't you have something else to do this morning?"

"Not at all," Nate said, grinning. One of his teeth was crooked, giving him a slightly feral look.

"What do you have there?" JoLynne asked, clutching her robe at the throat but leaning forward for a sniff. "Oh my god. That smells heavenly." She smiled up at Beau. "I'm going to get dressed."

Beau groaned inwardly, but stepped back. "Guess you're coming in."

Nate moved past him into the kitchen.

Beau closed the door and leaned against it, eyes closed, shaking his head. What the hell was Nate thinking, coming over early in the morning when he knew Beau had company?

In the kitchen, Nate poured himself a cup of coffee and sat down. Beau pulled out a chair across from him. "What gives?" he asked in a low voice.

"I saw the car."

"For most people, that would be a pretty good indicator that you need to mind your own business."

"Yep," Nate said, biting into a muffin and washing it down with coffee. "But you know me better than that. Oh, hello again."

He smiled at JoLynne, back in her jeans and blouse from yesterday, her hair freshly brushed and her face bright. She refilled her coffee cup and sat down next to Beau, bumping him happily with her shoulder.

With the three of them settled in around the kitchen table, mugs in hand, plates smeared with blueberry and cinnamon crumbs, Beau told himself to relax and enjoy the moment. JoLynne sat beside him, warm and friendly. Nate was showing his best side, keeping a lid on whatever mischief he was working up. It almost felt normal.

Then Nate stood to refill his coffee, and JoLynne glanced at his leg. Her expression turned sad.

Nate noticed and straightened slightly. "Little going-home present from Saddam," he said.

"I'm sorry you went through that," JoLynne said. "But thank you."

"I'd say 'my pleasure'," Nate said, "but I really can't." He winked, his voice suddenly polished, almost gentlemanly.

Beau went on alert.

"You were on Buck yesterday?" Nate asked. "He's a good horse. Real steady."

"He was perfect," JoLynne said, brushing a crumb from her mouth. "Very gentle and sure-footed. I could've kept going all day."

"He must have trusted you," Nate said. "Horses can tell."

"I grew up around them, but yesterday was the first time in years I've been on one, and we had so much fun. Beau showed me the creek. Beautiful."

"It definitely is," Nate said.

Beau watched them, uneasy. Nate, charming. JoLynne, relaxed. Something about it made his skin itch.

"Do you always bring your brother freshly baked pastries in the morning," JoLynne asked, teasing, "or is this a special occasion?"

Nate lifted his cup. "I'm just neighborly."

Beau shot him a look over the rim of his mug. Neighborly, my ass.

They made small talk for another few minutes. Weather, horses, trails. JoLynne complimented the ranch again, and Nate acted like he deserved the praise. Beau was about to interrupt, maybe suggest checking on the horses, when JoLynne spoke first.

"Do you still ride?" she asked. "If that's not too rude a question."

Nate went still. The corner of his mouth twitched. "I used to," he said flatly. "Before."

"I—I didn't think," JoLynne said.

"It's fine."

Silence settled between them.

Nate pushed his chair back and stood, taking his plate with him. "No harm. I've got things to do." He rinsed the plate and walked out without another word.

JoLynne turned to Beau. "I'm such an idiot."

"You didn't do anything wrong."

"Still." She stood up. "I should probably get going anyway. I've also got some things to do today."

Beau hesitated, but then he stood, too. He wanted to ask her to stick around for a while, maybe go for another ride, but she was already reaching for her purse.

He held the door open for her, and they stepped outside, the morning sun already warming the porch.

She paused, turning to him. "I really did have a great time yesterday," she said. "Riding down to the creek and meeting your friends. Dinner, and the rest." She smiled, suddenly embarrassed.

"Sorry about how it ended." He pulled her into his arms, rested his chin on her head, and closed his eyes. This woman. She was such a mix of guts and girlishness. She was mesmerizing.

In his arms, she gave a little snort of laughter. "Like you can control your brother. He's a grown man, and families can be complicated."

"Thanks for understanding." They exchanged a sweet kiss. "Can I call you later?"

"I'd like that."

She got into her car. When he closed the door, she started it and rolled down the window. "See you soon."

"Okay." He patted the door twice and stepped back.

Then she drove away, dust rising behind her tires.

Beau stood there for a moment, the air growing still around him. He wasn't alone, but it felt that way. As he cleaned up the kitchen and rinsed and loaded their dishes, he kept dawdling, lost in thought.

This wasn't productive. He had things to do, too.

Finishing with the kitchen, he went to the barn and threw himself into work. The horses nickered as he shoveled. Pretty soon, sweat soaked his shirt. The pitchfork scraped concrete as he moved to the next stall.

The barn door creaked open behind him. "Your girlfriend run off?"

"You saw her leave," Beau muttered, heaving another load of manure and straw.

"Why are you pissed at me? I didn't say anything wrong."

"You didn't have to."

Nate leaned against the wall. "What the hell's your problem?"

"You came over uninvited, hijacked breakfast, turned on the charm, then dropped a grenade."

"I didn't mean to," Nate said. "She asked. I answered."

Beau dumped another load into the wheelbarrow. "You make people feel like they stepped in it."

Nate shrugged. "She'll be back. Or maybe not. I don't really give a shit."

"Then why'd you come over?"

Nate did not answer. He brushed Shorty half-heartedly.

"You know," he said eventually, "she likes you."

Beau leaned on the handle of the pitchfork. The silence stretched. The work was never finished. Gates needed repair, the farrier should be scheduled. And his relationship with JoLynne was none of his brother's business. "I have work to do," he said.

Nate left. The barn fell silent again.

Beau stood alone, hay and heat pressing around him, the pitchfork stuck in the ground like a question he could not yet answer.

Seven

Driving home from Ramona, JoLynne felt downright giggly. She tried calling Vivian, but it went to voicemail, so she hung up. The drive was so pretty, and she was so happy, she almost didn't mind the missed connection, settling in for the trip back to Serena Cove with the upbeat radio station keeping pace with her mood.

Her night with Beau had been totally unexpected. She broke into a smile, remembering. When the sun had gone down and the air turned cold on the porch, and the late-harvest Zin was humming through her veins, Beau had threaded his fingers through hers, pulled her close, and brushed his lips against hers. She had closed her eyes and sighed, giving in to the inevitability of the night.

Thinking about it now, JoLynne shivered with delight. She felt brave going after what she wanted. Beau was everything good in a man—attractive, hard-working, funny, kind. She couldn't think of any other attributes that might be important. But then, what difference did it make? She wasn't in it for a relationship. For friends with benefits, he was perfect.

The thought of their hours together last night, getting to know each other by the light of a single candle, made her feel like singing. JoLynne felt more alive than she had in years, like a younger version of herself.

The phone rang, and she answered eagerly.

"I was in the shower when you called," said Vivian. "What's up?"

"You are not going to believe this," JoLynne said, launching into a description of the horseback ride, the beauty of the ranch, dinner with friends, and finally, the fact that she'd ended up spending the night with Beau. Throughout the telling, she sounded giddy.

When she finally wound down enough for her sister to get a word in, Vivian said, "I'm trying to process this. So, you went on a trail ride and wound up in his bed?"

"Well, yeah..." JoLynne laughed, realizing how it sounded. "But it's not like he's a stranger. We knew each other from before, because he worked with Gene."

"Okay, that makes more sense."

"I thought you'd be happier for me. Getting out there, and all that."

"I am happy for you," said Vivian, her tone brightening. "I was just surprised. Do you think you'll see him again?"

"Oh yeah," said JoLynne. "He definitely said he would call me."

There was a pause at the other end.

"Oh, come on," she said. "Even if he doesn't, I'm a big girl. It was fantastic, fabulous, and outstanding. But damn, I think I'm good for a while. This morning, I could hardly walk."

"TMI!" shouted Vivian, and they both laughed.

"Seriously," JoLynne said, "I'd be very disappointed if that was the last I ever saw of him, but I don't think that'll happen. He seemed really happy to have me around."

"I hope you're right," said Vivian. "You need more fun in your life."

"I do," said JoLynne. "And that's all it's going to be. Fun. Nothing serious. But you know what? I'm going to try to ride more often. Being out on that ranch, Viv... I felt like I was home, you know?" The sounds and smells of the ranch had brought back such rich memories, it had awakened something in her. And since she wasn't working fulltime, maybe she could find a way to duplicate the experience.

Well, not all of it, she thought with a wicked grin.

By the time she'd finished her story, the town sign for Serena Cove was already in view. Promising to call back in a few days with an update, JoLynne pulled into her driveway and gathered her things from the car. She had such a spring in her step, she figured if any neighbors were watching, they'd probably notice.

She slipped out of her clothes, dropped them in the hamper, and stepped into the shower. Feeling the hot spray bathe her face, JoLynne decided she had to upgrade her former impression of herself. She had never been all that brave around men. Flirtatious, sure, when circumstances arose. But throwing herself at Beau—she laughed to call it that—had felt like stepping out of the shadows and claiming what she wanted. She decided she enjoyed being this person, a woman who could just have quality casual sex whenever she needed it.

After getting dressed and having a light snack, she was still too full of energy to stay inside. Heading out the back door, she poked around in the small shed under the carport for gardening tools and got to work on the flowerbed around the front porch.

She kneeled in the dirt, the sun on her back, and thought about how badly the yard had fared while Gene was declining, but she'd had no energy to care. All she could do was look after his welfare and, to a lesser extent, her own. Those were hard years.

But now, Beau.

What did it mean that they'd skipped ahead to spending the night together on the first date? Would that be the end of it? Having gotten what he wanted, would he now ghost her?

But that was old thinking, from when she was young. Now, women were all about empowerment, and JoLynne had gotten what she wanted too. In fact, she had made the first move, impulsively going to see him at the warehouse.

Humming to herself, she got busy in her garden, clearing out the weeds and dead vegetation. When that was done, she would prepare the soil for new growth. Then, maybe tomorrow, visit the nursery in Serena Cove to pick up flowering plants. As she knelt, digging, pulling, and cutting, a dog barked nearby—short, excited, and familiar. JoLynne paused, sat back on her heels, and looked up just as a golf cart eased into her driveway. Cass waved from the front seat, with Sophie perched beside her like a little co-pilot.

"Morning, neighbor!"

JoLynne clambered to her feet with a grunt, her knees and hips complaining.

Cass tilted her head. "What's the matter?"

"Oh, I went horseback riding yesterday for the first time in years, and my body's complaining about it." JoLynne gestured to the rocking chairs on the porch. "What brings you out on this fine morning?"

"I'm on my way to the beach to go for a walk," said Cass, taking a chair. "I still can't believe we can do that whenever we want."

"It's a miracle," said JoLynne, nodding. "I don't care how bad this place gets—" she closed her eyes, raised her shoulders, and took in a deep breath, "it's worth it to be able to breathe that salt air, isn't it?"

She opened her eyes to see Cass studying her like a museum exhibit.

"You're awfully cheerful this morning."

"Um, yeah. Guess I slept good."

"Where'd you ride horses?" asked Cass.

"A friend's house."

"That man friend who came to see you?"

A car drove by, and JoLynne waved. "How's Gus?" she asked.

"He's great. I'm going with him on a run tomorrow."

"You say that like it's fun."

"It is," said Cass, her voice going all dreamy. "The truck has a sleeper in the back. We park off the road and build a fire. It's like camping."

"If you say so."

"Hey, I wonder if you could help me out. I was supposed to take Bernie shopping tomorrow because Leland hurt his ankle. Do you think you could do it?"

"Sure, I'll help. Give me Bernie's number and I'll call him this afternoon. Who's watching Sophie?"

"She comes along. She has her own little bed and everything." Cass stood up and tugged on the leash. "We should get going. Lots to do to get ready. Which reminds me. Diane's covering book club Wednesday while I'm gone. Don't let her chase anybody away, okay?"

"I'll keep an eye on her."

"Good." Cass waved as she and Sophie drove off.

JoLynne watched them go, happy to help. And then she remembered last night and grinned so wide her face hurt.

Ursula was not having the same kind of Sunday.

Amir had stopped by on one of his hurried visits. He reminded her he'd soon be flying to Istanbul alone, unless she changed her mind. He always said it so casually, but lately she'd started to wonder if he meant something more.

Bah! Her weakness again.

Then he kissed her cheek and left. She missed him the moment the door closed. Of course, they didn't call it a relationship. The pretense was casual. That was their unspoken agreement. She told herself it was for the best.

Amir had spent the last few years easing out of the more dangerous layers of his former work, whatever that meant now. Ursula hadn't asked. She didn't need to. Once upon a time, before the Iron Curtain fell, they'd worked in adjacent shadows. She knew the shape of the game, even if the rules had changed.

Lately, the world had flared again, and Amir had been "consulting." That was the word he used, as if he were advising a software company. She let him have the euphemism. The less said, the less denied.

Amir would never settle down. When he died, it would be in a conference room somewhere, mid-debrief. Hopefully, it would be that peaceful.

Their past had left them both with the same damage: a profound aversion to need. Need meant weakness. Neediness was a liability. Neither of them could risk it.

But that was then.

Lately, Ursula had been feeling off kilter. More than once, after he left, she found herself halfway to the phone, mentally composing a brief text.

It was absurd. She liked solitude. She liked being the kind of woman who kept a knife in her kitchen drawer sharp enough to cut bone.

But lately, she wondered what it might be like to lower her guard. Just slightly. To come in from the cold.

Then she imagined Amir at her breakfast table every morning, sharing the crossword, asking where she'd moved the cognac, and the thought made her recoil. No, that would ruin it. They needed the distance. They were held together by it.

Still, the house was too quiet after he left.

She took her Saab into the village for laundry detergent, a candle, and a small throw pillow she didn't need. Chatted briefly with the manager at the home goods store about a display of Turkish lamps.

The conversation was pleasant. Unimportant. But she lingered longer than necessary.

She told herself she was trying to be more of a homebody. It was a role she was learning to inhabit, however awkwardly, trying to envision a new future.

A future without Amir.

Eight

JoLynne drove Bernie to the grocery store, where he handed her his cane and climbed aboard one of the store's motorized scooters. Pushing a shopping cart, she had to hurry to keep up with the old man as he drove the thing like it was built for NASCAR.

It was their first outing together, and he was proving to be an interesting character. Pausing in the canned soup aisle, Bernie glared at the ceiling. "You hear that?"

JoLynne listened. "I hear music."

"Michael Bublé," he muttered. "Tryin' real hard to be Bobby Darin. Got a decent voice. But it ain't jazz. It's dinner music with a little popcorn."

She snorted. "That's harsh."

"I didn't say I don't like it," he shrugged, cruising wide around a paper towel display. "Just calling it what it is."

He beeped his scooter horn at a passing toddler and then glanced up at her. "By the way, thanks much for steppin' in to drive me today."

"No problem." She added cereal to the cart. "I'm happy to help any time Leland is under the weather."

Bernie tapped his temple. "I think old Lee might be milkin' it. You'd think he got hit by a train, the way he's acting all dramatic."

"Are you annoyed with him for being scared?" she asked.

"Heck no. After what happened, I'm just glad he came back."

Bernie's live-in helper, Leland, had been scared off by the previous HOA president, a petty tyrant who'd made threats of deportation. It had taken weeks to get Lee to return.

"How'd you convince him?" JoLynne asked.

Bernie stopped rolling. His face grew serious. "I told him anybody threatens him again, they'll have to go through me."

She glanced down at her wiry old neighbor. "Well, that should strike fear into the hearts of men."

"That's the idea."

He peeled off to flirt with the bakery lady, giving JoLynne a moment to glance at her phone. Nothing. Still no message from Beau. Not that she was expecting roses or a sonnet. But after a night like that? A text wouldn't kill him.

She dropped her phone back into her bag before she could overthink it.

At checkout, Bernie cruised on ahead while JoLynne loaded the bags. After he climbed into her car, she returned the motorized cart to the store.

"You pretty busy these days?" he asked as she backed out.

"Not too bad. Why do you ask?"

"Well, I don't like to meddle in other people's business," he began, "but there's a buddy of mine who lives on the street behind me. Leonard. He ain't doing so good."

"Okay," she said, steering toward the exit. "And?"

"And he needs to get to the clinic in town, but his doctor just took away his keys. He doesn't drive anymore."

"You're asking me to take him?"

Bernie brightened. "Now that's a great idea."

"What about Uber? Or Dial-a-Ride?"

"They're fine," he said, waving it off. "But it's different when you know the person. Leonard'd feel better if someone stayed with him in the waiting room. Just in case the doc needs to explain something or whatever."

She frowned. "Are we talking one visit or a regular thing? Because I need to look for work."

"It'd only be part of the time, and he'd pay you under the table. Keep you busy while you're lookin' for something more permanent."

She drove on without answering.

"Think about it," he said. "You'd be helping somebody and makin' a few bucks besides. What's not to like?" He pulled a bent business card from his wallet and set it in the console. The original info was scratched out, with a new number written in pen.

"He has a card?" JoLynne squinted down at it.

"He used to work for the government," Bernie said. "His doctor appointment's tomorrow. Give him a call if you can."

After dropping off Bernie and putting away his groceries, she pulled into her driveway and stared at the number scribbled on Leonard's card. A couple of bucks under the table was better than nothing. She tapped the call button.

The next morning, JoLynne parked in front of a yellow mobile home with its paint peeling, wind chimes jangling from a crooked hook on the porch. She knocked on the screen door, heard a voice call, "It's open!" and let herself in.

His living room was bright, with the shades open to let in the sunlight. A comfortable old recliner stood next to the wall. Above it hung an American flag and a wall-mounted glass case of service medals.

Leonard stood leaning on a cane. "I'm ready," he said, stepping out without waiting for help.

She stayed close behind as he navigated the front steps, careful not to hover, and then drove in silence, giving him space.

At the clinic's front desk, Leonard leaned his cane against the counter. "I'm here for my appointment," he told the receptionist.

"First visit?" the woman asked. When he nodded, she shoved a clipboard through the slot. "Fill it all out. Be sure to do front and back."

He tucked it under his arm and shuffled to the seat JoLynne had saved him.

"I'm supposed to fill all this junk out," he muttered, squinting at the fine print. "Should've brought my magnifying glass."

She leaned over. "Want me to read it?"

"If you wouldn't mind."

She read the questions one by one in a low voice, watching him scribble answers in a spidery scrawl. Every few lines, he rubbed his eyes. The memory of Gene's worsening eyesight flickered through her, how angry and lost he'd been during those months. Frailty made everything harder.

A few minutes later, someone came and got Leonard. JoLynne looked at her phone, prepared for it to take a long time. She noted with annoyance that Beau still hadn't gotten in touch.

After a while, a familiar voice cut through the noise. "JoLynne?" Teresa, the nurse-practitioner who lived near Cass, crossed the waiting room. "Did you bring Leonard in?" Teresa asked, dropping into the seat beside her.

"I drove him," JoLynne said. "Is there a problem?"

Teresa nodded. "Leonard says he has a daughter, but when I asked him if he'd be willing to give me her contact information, he closed down. Do you know anything about her? It would be helpful if I could get in touch with her."

"I'm sorry. I don't really know him that well. We just met," said JoLynne.

"So frustrating." Teresa rubbed her forehead. "There are so many elders in the park with no one to help them. Well, thanks for getting him here."

JoLynne watched as Teresa disappeared through the doors. The air in the waiting room felt heavier than before.

She was glad to help, and it took so little effort. If she could afford to, she'd do it for free.

Not long afterward, Leonard reappeared, moving slowly but upright, his cane tapping with measured precision. "If it's not too much trouble," he said, "I'd appreciate a quick stop at the pharmacy."

"Happy to," said JoLynne.

Leonard handed her a list and a credit card.

When they got back to his house, she followed him up the steps with his pharmacy bag. In the living room, he thanked her again and peeled off several bills from a fat wad of twenties.

"This is too much," JoLynne objected.

"You were a big help," said Leonard. "Anyway, I'm old, not poor."

"I didn't mean anything."

He waved off her concern. "I wonder if you would be available to take me grocery shopping next week."

"Of course." They agreed on a date and time, and JoLynne let herself out. As she walked to the car, she realized something was tugging at her thoughts. First Bernie, and now Leonard. She wondered if there were more people in the park who could use her help. Neither of the men had asked for much. Just a ride, a little time, and some minor assistance, which JoLynne could provide.

Getting back into her car, she pulled out her phone again. Still nothing from Beau. Was she supposed to call him? How were things done these days? She didn't know. She tucked it into her purse, slower this time.

Well, she was an adult, and so was he. He'd either reach out, or he wouldn't. Either way, she had things to do and places to be.

Humming to the radio, JoLynne headed for home. Michael Bublé was crooning again. Dinner music with popcorn, she thought, smiling as she turned up the volume.

Nine

B eau shook his head in frustration, gripping the hand radio. "No, it's too early. He's not cleared for the forklift."

Striding the catwalk outside his office, keeping watch over a ballet of moving pallets, forklifts, and motorized dollies, he listened as his underling argued. Closing his eyes and telling himself to be patient, Beau explained his reasoning over the radio.

"Listen, Joaquin, I understand. I know you need help, but the guy's only shadowed twice. It's too tight down there. And where the hell is Marta?"

Beau rubbed his temples as the radio squawked back at him. Every channel buzzed with another small fire, another problem to solve. Someone had clocked out early. A pallet was labeled wrong. One of the new kids clipped a support post, and the team was down there assessing damage and culpability.

He pressed the button again and again, directing Smith to go here and Aguilera to go there, inventing solutions on the fly and quelling disputes.

There were times when he strode through Acme Logistics with a straight spine and a smile on his face, knowing he was good at warehouse management, knowing he had earned the position through merit and hard work.

The turnover rate among his people was low for the industry, and he took genuine pleasure in teaching and training them to reach new heights. He had an innate sense that he was the right guy for the job.

But there were other times, like today, when Beau wondered what the hell management had been thinking when they promoted him to this position in the first place.

And then things got worse when his phone rang.

Nate only called when he needed something, when something was going wrong at the ranch. He didn't seem to understand that Beau had a full-time job.

Or care.

"What?" Beau said, irritation leaching into his voice.

"You don't have to be snotty," Nate replied.

"I've got a ton of shit going on," Beau said. "What do you need?"

"The neighbor's goats broke through the south fence. I know we talked to Cora about it, but she let her fencing go after that storm last month, and they took advantage of it."

Beau pinched the bridge of his nose. "How bad is it?"

"Not good," Nate said. "They're in the back field, chewing on tarp straps and climbing the tractor. One of them got stuck halfway up the compost pile and panicked. I had to crawl under the fence to keep it from snapping a leg, and now my good knee's locking up."

Beau sighed, already turning away from the mezzanine. "Have you talked to Cora?"

"I tried. She didn't pick up."

Beau exhaled, glancing down at the warehouse floor. Work was moving at the same pace, but now two guys were arguing, and someone was waving a clipboard in the air. He turned from one emergency to another.

"How many goats are out there?"

"Five. No, wait. Six. One just climbed into the garden, and it's eating your lettuce."

"Jesus." Beau looked up at the ceiling. "If I left right now, it'd take me about an hour to get there. And I can't leave right now. There's nothing you can do?"

"Brother, right now I've got my leg elevated and I'm hoping I don't need to go to urgent care."

"All right," Beau said. "Let me see if I can get someone to cover and then I'll try to head home."

The line went dead.

Beau stared at his phone before shoving it into his pocket. Below him, a case was dropped, and the sharp crack echoed across the warehouse. No one even looked up.

He clicked the radio. "Ramirez, you've got Receiving until I get back. Marta's still AWOL, and if that pipe shipment comes early, text me and stall. Do not sign anything until I check it."

Ramirez confirmed. Beau ducked into his office, explained quickly to his secretary, grabbed his keys and the tablet he used for field notes, then jogged down the back stairs and out into the sun.

It was too damn bright. Too damn hot.

Fifteen minutes after he hung up with Nate, he climbed into his truck, slammed the door harder than necessary, and started the engine. Soon he was stuck in commuter traffic, inching along toward home. There was an accident along the roadway, forcing cars into a single lane. Time was ticking away. By the time he got home, the emergency would either be resolved or past fixing.

Blinking at the glare off the hood and waiting for traffic to clear, his phone lit up again. Beau punched the speaker. "Yeah."

"You can stand down. I got ahold of Cora."

Beau's hands tightened on the wheel. "What?"

"She got home, got my message, found some helpers, and they're in the process of chasing the goats back over to her side of the fence," Nate said. "So you can stay at work."

Beau stared through the windshield.

"Look," Nate said, his tone shifting slightly. "I was in a jam. I didn't call for fun."

"Fine," Beau said. "Glad it's handled, but I already left work."

"Since you're on the road anyway," said Nate, "you mind picking up dinner on your way home?"

Beau ended the call without a response.

He should be able to rely more on Nate, but Beau was not about to leave the ranch in his brother's hands, no matter how hard it was. Maintaining the place and preserving his family's legacy—that was all-important.

And Nate could not help what happened to him in the Gulf. He'd done his patriotic duty. The two brothers were supposed to go in together, but Beau, with faulty peripheral vision, wasn't able to enlist. That wasn't his fault, but the guilt weighed on him.

It would be easier if there were someone to blame, someone to point at and yell, *My life is shit and it's all because of you.*

But there wasn't. It was just life.

Resigned, he put in a call to the Italian place near home, ordering takeout to be ready in a half-hour. He might be pissed at Nate, but they still had to eat, and Beau had no interest in whatever his brother might try to whip up. Could be boxed mac and cheese or a can of soup. Not appealing.

Still, Nate's cinnamon rolls last Sunday had been a nice surprise. An honest offering. Nate had many shortcomings, but he was not a girlfriend stealer.

Of course, JoLynne was the farthest thing from a girlfriend.

Beau had to face the truth. Unless he reached out to her, what they had was essentially a one-night stand. The only way to make it right was to try to see her again. To develop an actual friendship. That was what he'd ask for, if he were free to ask for anything.

He should have called by now, but what was the point? Between the ranch and the job, he had little to offer. No time for dates, no matter how wonderful the woman.

He felt so drawn to her. Not just physically, but emotionally, in the sense that they understood each other. Her familiarity with ranch life, her ease in the saddle, her affection for the horses. Watching her pull Buck's muzzle close and lean her forehead against his long nose, her eyes closed, the longing in her was almost visceral. She was so comfortable at the ranch and had told him how much it stirred memories of her home in Montana.

But their friendship had to end where it was. Better for her.

He drove on until the restaurant appeared on his right. He pulled into the lot, went inside for his food, carried the order out to the truck, and set it on the passenger seat. Leaning against the open door, keys dangling from his hand, metal still hot from the drive, he wondered why he was reluctant to head back to the ranch.

Routine had begun to feel heavier than he liked.

His phone buzzed in his back pocket. What the hell now? He dug it out, cursing.

JOLYNNE COLTRANE.

Beau blinked and answered so fast he nearly dropped it. "Hey."

"Hey yourself," she said. "Busy?"

He exhaled, smiling despite himself. "I'm actually just on my way home."

"Cutting out early, huh?"

"It's a long story," he said. "I'm grabbing dinner for me and Nate. What's up?"

"Well," she said. "I've been thinking about last Saturday."

His heart gave a ridiculous little jolt. "The trail ride?"

"Mm hmm. And the steak. And the swing. And all the other parts of it."

Beau's voice dropped. "Me too."

The silence stretched between them. An eighteen-wheeler rumbled past on the highway. When it was quiet again, JoLynne said, "Anyway. I had a very nice time." She paused, and he heard her take a breath. "I'd do it again," she said.

Throwing caution to the wind, Beau told her the truth. "I'd like that very much," he said, "but I worry that there'll be times I'm just not available to you, and I don't want you to think anything bad when that happens."

"If we're being honest with each other, there's something I want to be upfront about." Her voice was firmer now. "I had a great time. I really did. And I'd like to do it again. You seem like a genuinely nice guy, and I don't want to mislead you about my true intentions. Which are just to have fun and not get attached. If that's not too self-serving."

Relieved, Beau waited a second as if weighing her announcement. Then he said, "This is really about the horses, isn't it?"

She laughed. "You figured me out. I'm just pretending to like you to get to Hashtag."

"Thought so. He's the real attraction. I'm just the guy who hauls hay."

"You're a decent hay hauler," she said. "But this works better for me if we keep it light. I don't want to give you the wrong idea."

He tilted his head back, feeling the heat of the metal. "If it makes you feel better, I haven't had time to get any ideas, between my job and the ranch."

"Everything okay?"

"Now it is."

"Good." Her smile carried through the line, and the silence between them felt warm.

"So," she said. "If you don't have lunch plans next Saturday—"

"I don't."

"I was thinking maybe a picnic on the beach. The water's warming up, and it should be nice."

"That's a lie," he said. "That water never warms up."

"True. But it feels so good once you're out and drying off in the sun."

They talked logistics, said goodbye, and hung up. Beau climbed into his pasta-scented truck and started the engine, grinning like a fool.

Landry, you're so screwed, he thought.

But he didn't care.

Ten

Walking to the clubhouse on the foggy evening, JoLynne had Beau on her mind. After impulsively inviting him to a beach picnic, just the two of them, the good part was thinking about enjoying lunch, flirting, possibly moving from the beach chairs to a blanket on the sand, and whatever the evening might bring.

The bad part was worrying about what her house would look like through his eyes when they returned from the beach. Because of course she'd be bringing him home.

Although she'd tried to fix it up, it still looked pretty shabby. When she bought it five years ago, she'd made little improvements here and there. JoLynne wasn't made of money, so she pinched pennies and took it slowly, savoring whatever small changes she could afford. Which hadn't amounted to much. The house still looked pretty sad.

Still, she was feeling a strange lightness.

She stuck her hands in her pockets, smiling to herself. Her evening with Beau had rebalanced something in her. She'd never envisioned retirement as a time to be swinging from the chandeliers, but apparently a little disruption had been just what she needed. It had righted her ship, helped her feel normal again.

With a few minutes to spare before book club, she headed toward the bench overlooking the ocean. She was surprised to see Ursula sitting there and wondered whether the other woman would mind company. JoLynne was introverted, but Ursula operated on an entirely different level. Despite offering her backyard for group gatherings, she always seemed distant, aloof, deliberately at arm's length.

At the bench, JoLynne hesitated.

"You can sit," Ursula said without looking up.

JoLynne sat. Wordlessly, they watched the fog swirl in the last light of day. Seagulls circled overhead, calling to each other.

"Did you read the book?" JoLynne asked.

"It was not to my taste."

"But you're still going tonight?"

"I am committed to attending."

"Me, too," said JoLynne. "Sometimes, you just have to make an effort, even if you'd rather stay home by yourself."

Ursula pulled her jacket tighter. "I have always treasured my privacy and independence," she said. "After growing up in East Berlin, one does."

"I'd imagine that's true."

"However, I wonder if one might take it too far. Sometimes, I wonder what the goal was."

"A very peaceful house?"

Ursula looked away. "A very quiet heart."

They sat together in silence. In the distance, waves crashed on a shoreline hidden in fog.

"I'm starting to think it might be healthier to let some regular humans in," JoLynne said. "If I'm careful."

"I wish you good luck with that." Ursula looked at JoLynne very seriously, and then, just barely, a smile curved her lips.

JoLynne laughed, and to her surprise, Ursula chuckled too. It was the first time she'd ever seen the woman show a hint of humor.

Before JoLynne could respond, Diane's voice reached them through the fog.

"Book club is starting! Everyone? We're waiting."

JoLynne looked at Ursula. "Ready?"

Ursula made a slight gesture as if to say *you first*, and they headed for the clubhouse. Passing through the chain-link gate, they met Diane standing in the doorway, arms folded.

"What's the problem?" JoLynne asked.

In a low voice, Diane replied, "This was supposed to be a women's book club."

"I don't think that was ever really stated," said Kellie, the dog groomer, arriving from the parking lot.

"And it's only for residents," Diane added pointedly.

JoLynne ushered Kellie through the door. Then she glared at Diane. "Cass wanted you to run the meeting, not run people off. Men are welcome, and so are non-residents if they have friends in the park."

"Fine," said Diane. "Don't blame me if it goes off the rails."

Just then, Chuck, the handyman, walked up. He wore a long-sleeved gray Henley, dark Levi's, and a nice watch.

"I brought refreshments," he said, extending a grocery bag toward Diane.

"God," she huffed, turning her back on them and going inside. Chuck and JoLynne looked at each other, bemused. Then Chuck dove through the door, following Diane.

Teresa was already inside, flipping through her annotated paperback. A couple of vacationers from the short-term units hovered near the door, as if unsure whether they'd wandered into something private.

At the round table in the corner, Chuck set the bag down. From it, he pulled out three bottles of wine—two whites and a red—followed by a package of tiny paper cups.

"What do you think you're doing?" asked Diane. "We're not supposed to drink in here."

"We're not drinking." Chuck cradled one bottle against his chest and twisted a corkscrew. "We're tasting. I picked these up last time I was cruising around the Four Corners area. They're fairly interesting."

"But you can't serve alcohol in the—"

POP.

The cork flew out, and Chuck stood there looking at her, all innocence. "It's open now," he said, pouring small amounts of the first white into the tiny cups.

The Thursday night Serena Cove Book and Wine Tasting Club was off and running.

JoLynne found an empty seat next to Teresa.

"I'm glad you're here," Teresa said. "I wanted to ask you something about Leonard."

Kellie stopped in front of them, offering each a cup of wine. Teresa shrugged and accepted, and JoLynne took a sip.

"Folks, this is a chardonnay from the Verde Valley, up near Sedona. Not as famous as Napa, but don't sleep on it. It's got high elevation, volcanic soil, and just enough weird energy from the Sedona vortexes to keep the grapes interesting."

"Thing is," Teresa said, tossing back her wine, "a lot of our services could be handled right here in the park. Especially for people like Leonard."

JoLynne raised an eyebrow. "I think you're supposed to taste it."

"Right. Forgot." Teresa accepted a second pour and turned back. "So anyway, I was thinking, what if we did more publicity? Cass said something about upgrading the park's email messaging system."

JoLynne nodded, intrigued. "I like that. But good luck pulling people away from their daytime game shows."

"Now, this next selection," said Chuck, "is a chardonnay from the same vineyard—new grafts, old vines. What do you think?"

Teresa downed it in one gulp. "I think Leonard could use more attention. And so could the rest of them. All the frail elders in the park."

"People, people!" Diane's voice cut in. "Now that you're all good and lubricated, how about we talk about the book?"

"We can talk and taste at the same time, can't we?" Chuck raised the third bottle.

Diane dropped her head back and muttered a curse. Then she held out her cup.

Kellie came around with a fresh bottle.

"Leonard is like a lot of them," Teresa said, holding out her cup. "He has a daughter, but she's unreliable. No real options for him. That's all I'm saying."

"Thanks, Kel," said JoLynne. She took a sip of her wine. It was so rich and smooth, she wanted to order a case of it. But Teresa was waiting. "Let's talk to Cass," JoLynne said. "She might be able to help."

By now the room was unraveling. The noise level rose, accompanied by frequent laughter.

Diane, increasingly annoyed, tried to wrangle them back. "Can we please discuss the actual novel?"

"This one was dull," said Roni. "How about we get something with a little spice?"

Her boyfriend, Jordan the fire chief, took her hand and pulled her close with a wolfish grin.

Diane threw up her hands and slumped near the wine table. Immediately, Chuck appeared beside her, holding the back of a chair as if seating her at a fine restaurant.

"Can I offer you something else?" he asked.

"Might as well top it off." She held out her little cup. "Did you get the nighttime pool lighting installed yet?"

"I did, and it's very attractive. It's dark now," he said. "Want to see?"

"Why not?" They slipped out the door together. JoLynne watched them go, and saw Chuck's hand resting lightly on Diane's lower back.

Looked like she wasn't the only one howling at the moon.

Cass sat down next to her, wine in hand. "Happy chaos, right?"

JoLynne smiled. "We wanted social. We're definitely getting it."

Later, back at her place, Ursula flicked on a single lamp. The living room was dim. The corners held shadows. On the small table by the couch sat a neat stack of untouched magazines and a pile of unopened mail. She hadn't bothered with dinner. Sometimes a boiled egg or a piece of toast was enough. Tonight at the "book club," she'd enjoyed a little wine. That would do.

Moving through her routine automatically, she locked the door, folded a throw blanket, and changed into nightclothes—a threadbare T-shirt from an intelligence conference in Prague and the same gray sweatpants she'd worn for years. Her slippers made no sound on the carpet.

Down the hall, the bathroom was spare and orderly. Everything in its place. She brushed her teeth, rinsed, and flicked off the light.

And then she paused outside the spare bedroom, which served as the library and office. Against her own will, she opened her laptop without sitting down, intending only to check the news. But her fingers moved automatically to her inbox.

One new message.

Her breathing quickened.

The subject line read: You Would Like This

Ursula stared at the screen before clicking. The photo was recent, of Amir smiling against a twilight skyline. The Bosphorus stretched behind him, soft as smoke. He stood on a stone balcony, one arm extended toward the view as if offering it to someone. The wind had pressed his shirt flat to his body, his silver and gray hair tousled, his smile real and unbothered.

There was no message. Just the photo. She slapped the laptop shut with one hand. Back in the bedroom, she turned down the covers and lay flat, arms stiff at her sides.

In the picture, Amir was laughing. But that was deceptive. He moved through the world without leaving footprints. He was quiet, self-contained, dangerous in a way most people missed.

Now, this. The invitations. The photos. He kept reaching out while she remained silent.

That was the trouble with Amir, who saw straight through her and still didn't flinch. He didn't push because he knew better. But lately, he had been reaching out more often.

She shifted. Tried to readjust the pillow. Couldn't get it right. Pulled the quilt up. Threw it down again.

The last time she was in Istanbul, she played the part of a tourist while working. She loved the city and vowed to return. That had never happened.

Now, Amir's invitation lingered in her mind. She could go. She wanted to go. But she hadn't bought the ticket.

Amir was on assignment. She didn't want to fly halfway around the world just to sit alone while he worked. Besides, she was determined to fully inhabit her world here on this California beach.

JoLynne had been right. The two of them had everything they needed right here at home.

She turned again, once more, and gave herself up to a fitful sleep.

Eleven

JoLynne and Beau made their way across the warm sand, with him
lugging the cooler, her carrying two fold-up chairs and a lightweight
umbrella. Beau was wearing board shorts and a nicely fitting blue tee shirt.
JoLynne was feeling unexpectedly girly. After years of caregiving frumpery,
Vivian's influence was clearly having an effect. After careful consideration,
she put on a cute cover-up and floppy sun hat from their most recent
cruise.

"I think we're good here," she said, setting her things down.

"Perfect," he said, easing the cooler onto the sand and giving his back a
stretch.

She unfolded the chairs and then brushed her hands off on the sides
of her turquoise cover-up. Beau glanced over, his gaze lingering just a
second longer than necessary. Suddenly self-conscious, JoLynne grabbed
the umbrella and tried to shove it into the sand.

He reached around behind her. "Let me," he said, his voice low in her
ear.

JoLynne didn't move right away. His nearness sent a tingle up her spine,
and she wanted to note it. Enjoy it.

But he needed room to work. Reluctantly, she stepped aside and let him take the umbrella.

He anchored it deeply in the sand, his forearms flexing just enough to be distracting.

They sat in their chairs. JoLynne closed her eyes and let her head drop back. Soon, she'd offer him the lunch she'd prepared, of fried chicken, potato salad, and wine. But just for a second, she wanted to enjoy the moment.

You couldn't ask for a nicer day. The fog had burned off, leaving the sky as blue as a robin's egg, with fluffy white clouds scudding past. Overhead, a small prop plane flew by pulling a banner; something about tequila. Joggers trotted by, and the surf rolled in with a steady hush. The music playing from a nearby speaker was unexpectedly catchy.

"Listen," she said. "Isn't that great? I'm wondering who it is."

"Beyoncé," he said. "That's from her Texas album." When she looked at him in surprise, he shrugged. "The horses like it, and I have to admit, it helps the work go faster in the barn."

"Okay, I'm going to have to catch up with you," she said.

"Good luck with that," he said, laughing when she poked him in the arm. "How about a little swim before lunch?" he asked, already standing and brushing the sand from his hands.

JoLynne dug her toes into the sand. "I'm good."

"You don't want to get in the water?"

"Maybe later," she said.

"I'm picking up on more than just simple hesitation." Beau grasped the arm of her beach chair and shook it a little. She looked up at him, silent.

"What are you not telling me?"

"I can't swim," she admitted.

"Are you serious? How can you live in Southern Cal and not know how to swim?"

"I just don't. I never learned growing up, and then I was working all the time, and it just never happened. But you go ahead."

"At least get in up to your knees. Come on."

JoLynne hesitated. It wasn't just that she didn't want to drown. She felt awkward about removing her cover-up. Underneath, she was wearing a pretty one-piece, also from the cruise. But in the glare of the midday light, she was uncomfortably aware of her age, her skin, and everything that entailed. Sure, he had already seen her naked, but that was by candlelight. This was in bright sunshine.

While she hesitated, shifting weight from one foot to the other, Beau gathered the back of his tee shirt and pulled it over his head and off his arms, treating her to the sight of his bare torso.

He glanced up and caught her staring. "What?"

JoLynne shook her head, bemused. "You're looking good, Mr. Landry."

"You too, Ms. Coltrane." He stood. "Ready?"

"As I'll ever be," she grumbled, slipping off her cover-up and tossing it on the chair.

He held out his hand. She took it, half-amused, half-stunned, to find herself walking the beach, nearly naked, in broad daylight at the age of sixty-three, and with a very good-looking, slightly younger man. A man who, aside from one unforgettable night, was still basically a stranger.

At the waterline, JoLynne stopped. Beau kept hold of her hand.

"Come on."

"It's freezing," she whimpered, her ankles already aching.

"Look at all the people swimming," he said. "Just come in up to your waist. I'll keep hold of you, and you'll get used to it. It'll be fun."

"Fun." But she let him haul her into knee-deep water which, when a wave swelled, would reach her waist and make her clench her teeth so as not to scream. The Pacific was no joke. Despite the name, it was one of the unruliest oceans on the planet, and even along the California coast, always chilly.

Although, as cold as it was, Beau's hand was very warm, his grip reassuring.

"Doing better?"

"Yeah, a little," she said. Because damn if he wasn't right. After a few minutes of torture, the water didn't feel as cold anymore. At least on the part of her body that was submerged. They stood holding onto each other, pushed about by the momentum of the waves. The cold didn't matter as much now. His hands were warm and steady, and he wasn't letting go.

JoLynne began to relax. "This isn't as horrible anymore."

"Told you," he said, watching her. "If you want, I can help you try floating a little."

She met his eyes, and something warm passed between them. She knew he would look out for her. With Beau, she felt safe.

"Maybe another time," she said, chickening out. "But you go."

"If you wouldn't mind? I'd like to paddle around a little."

She made a shooing motion and stepped back so as not to get sucked in. Then she watched as he dove under a breaker, disappearing as the wave broke over him and then waving at her from the other side. She waved back, and he dove again, looking for all the world like a frolicking marine mammal.

For the first time in her life, JoLynne thought she understood what people liked about swimming. There was a pool right up on the bluff, at the clubhouse. Wouldn't swimming in that pool represent a big move forward in her growth journey?

She'd have to think about that.

But right now, she was cold. With one last glimpse of Beau churning through the water like a dolphin, she headed toward their picnic site. There, she grabbed a towel, drying off and scanning the area where Beau had been. As a non-swimmer, she still didn't quite trust that he would be okay and was relieved when he turned back toward her.

When he emerged from the dark blue-green water, sparkling rivulets running over his chest and tracing down his stomach, she had to remind herself to breathe. All she could think about was what might happen later.

She handed him a towel. He took it with a murmur of thanks, rubbed the water from his face and hair, then slung it around his shoulders as he sat beside her. "What's for lunch?"

"Fried chicken and potato salad," she said, serving it up. "I made it last night."

He handed her a napkin and then took a bite of a drumstick, and then another, a little hum of satisfaction escaping his lips. "This is incredible," Beau said.

"It's pretty much idiot-proof," she laughed.

They ate from paper plates, using the cooler between them as a makeshift table. JoLynne poured from a small bottle of wine she'd tucked into the cooler, pleased with how everything had come together. If this was her new life, she liked it very much.

When they finished up and put away their plates and napkins, Beau gave her a lazy smile and leaned back. "Thank you. That was great."

"You're welcome."

They kicked back, full and content, toes dug into the sand. For a while, they just sat, watching the waves roll in, the sound of kids laughing in the distance. The sun warmed their shoulders. The breeze ruffled the edges of the umbrella. Music played nearby, and waterbirds skittered across the wet sand, hunting for a meal.

JoLynne glanced at him out of the corner of her eye. There was something about the peaceful, easy silence between them that drew her to him like a magnet. Beau looked over and smiled as if he were thinking the same thing. It did something to her breathing.

She refilled her cup and tilted the bottle toward him. He didn't take it right away. Instead, he looked at her like he wanted to say something else.

"Do you want more?" she asked.

He hesitated. "I can't. I have to drive."

She paused, lowering the bottle slightly. "Drive?"

He sighed. "Yeah. I'm really sorry, but I have to get back. The farrier had a cancellation this afternoon, and he's hard to book."

JoLynne set the bottle back in the cooler, hiding her annoyance and disappointment. After all the fantasizing about him coming back to her house for the evening—

He reached over and traced a finger up her arm. "I really am sorry. I'd hoped we could have dinner together."

"It's okay," she said breezily. "We didn't really discuss it ahead of time."

"You know how much I enjoy spending time with you."

"Yeah." She looked out at the waves. For a moment, the disappointment stung.

But then she smiled to herself, thinking what a wanton woman she was turning into. Well, it was his fault. And, okay, years of deprivation.

"Really, I had a good day anyway," she said.

"I did, too. I just hate that the ranch takes so much time that I truly wish I could spend with you." He pulled her in with one arm, apologizing. It was sweet.

As they packed up, she said, "You know, I could help."

"Help?"

"At the ranch."

He gave her a skeptical look. "It's not really your problem."

"It'd be an opportunity. I could ride Buck and Shorty once in a while, feed and curry them, whatever you need."

He shook his head. "That's a long way to drive just to do a few chores."

"You're not listening to me," she said, tugging on his arm. "Going riding with you brought back a lot of memories, good ones, and I realized how much I missed it. To spend time out there on the ranch, you'd be doing me a favor."

"I can't let you do that."

She let it go. There was probably no point in trying to change his mind.

As they picked up their things and walked back toward the truck, JoLynne watched him load everything, not letting her help. He was always trying to make things easier for everybody.

Why not himself?

She said nothing more, just climbed into the passenger seat. If he wouldn't let her help, fine. But that didn't mean he didn't need it.

And maybe he didn't have to carry all of it alone.

Beau flipped the visor down, but the late afternoon sun still caught the corners of his vision, turning everything sharp and hard. He couldn't stop thinking about JoLynne's face when he said he had to leave. She'd been bummed out, even though she tried to hide it.

It wasn't a lie about the farrier. But it was a convenient out, and he'd taken it. He would have loved to spend the evening with JoLynne and wake up beside her, but it wouldn't be fair to lead her on. And for her to work at the ranch like hired help, that just felt wrong.

But who was he lying to now? The absolute truth was that Beau was scared. He couldn't afford to take the risk that the text would ever surface. And it could, even though Gene was dead and Beau was innocent.

"I see the way you look at my wife." Gene had said it to Beau a decade ago as the two of them sat in the bleachers at the company's annual softball tournament. "It's written all over your sad mug."

"You're hallucinating," Beau had replied, honestly surprised that Gene would think that of him.

Years later, Gene followed up with the damning text.

She's got a good house, warm bed. Somebody's going to get her. Might as well be you.

Disgusted, Beau had deleted it from his phone, but it was burned into his memory along with guilt for not responding more strongly.

Because what had he sent back?

Not: *Go to hell.*

Not: *Don't talk about her like she's your property.*

Just: "Let's not talk about this."

That was all.

Not a defense of JoLynne. Not even a refusal. Just a man ducking his head and hoping the storm would blow over.

He hated that text more than he'd hated Gene in that moment. Hated his own weakness.

Now JoLynne was starting to laugh again. She was opening up, talking about coming to the ranch, and all he could think was that she didn't know what Gene had said, or that Beau hadn't stood up for her.

Maybe she never would.

Twelve

At the entrance to the nature preserve, Leonard rolled down his window before JoLynne could reach for her wallet.

"I've got it," he said, already pulling out a twenty from his billfold.

The attendant leaned forward, squinting into the vehicle. "Good morning," she said brightly.

Leonard handed over the money with a small nod. "For two."

The gate arm lifted. As JoLynne drove them in, the world changed. Low coastal scrub gave way to dense brush, eucalyptus, and tall Monterey pines that bowed and whispered in the breeze. The narrow road twisted through light and shadow, then opened onto a parking area edged by green. The air was thick with wild fennel and warm pine resin. Somewhere downhill, a creek gurgled on its way to the sea.

JoLynne turned off the engine. "This okay?"

Leonard looked out through the windshield for a long moment. "It's better than okay," he said. Then he smiled faintly. "Let's get the hell out of the car."

She opened the hatch and pulled out his walker, then his satchel, which he insisted on bringing even though it held almost nothing. Leonard shifted his weight and got out carefully, gripping the door before moving to the walker.

JoLynne stayed close but let him set the pace. She'd promised to take him out today for some fresh air. With his physical limitations, these outings didn't happen often. He'd had a quick checkup at the clinic earlier, and when she'd suggested the preserve afterward, he hadn't hesitated.

They made their way slowly toward the visitor center. "Do you want to do any shopping?" she asked as they stepped inside.

He shook his head. "No thanks. I would just like to go out back and enjoy the view."

She held the door for him, and they stepped out onto the rear patio.

Leonard chose a chair at a proper table, one with arms and an upright seat, easier for him than the lounges. JoLynne sat beside him. For a while, neither of them spoke. Below, a gravel trail curled through the brush toward the creek. Butterflies flitted through shafts of light. The eucalyptus creaked softly in the breeze.

"Now that I'm smelling lunch, I'm feeling hungry." She glanced toward the café window. "Want to split a roast beef sandwich?"

"That sounds good. And perhaps a lemonade?" he added, looking hopeful.

"You got it." She headed inside and placed their order. A few minutes later, she returned with two halves of a roast beef sandwich and two small lemonades. They sat in comfortable silence, gazing across the downhill slope toward the ocean.

JoLynne had to admit she was glad Leonard had agreed to come here. It really was beautiful. She was still learning how to relax, how to be still without waiting for the next crisis.

"What's new in your life?" he asked. "Anything interesting?"

She told him about the beach picnic the day before, admitting to her embarrassment over not knowing how to swim.

"You know who does?" Leonard said, chewing thoughtfully. "Ursula. She used to swim for East Germany when she was a teenager."

JoLynne blinked at him. "You've got to be kidding me."

"I'm not kidding. That woman is amazing. She comes over every Tuesday and plays chess with me."

JoLynne leaned back. "Wonders will never cease."

They chatted easily for the next forty-five minutes, but when she noticed his eyes drooping, JoLynne suggested they head home. The drive back was quiet. Leonard dozed most of the way, and she was pleased to have given him this outing.

And per her list on the fridge, she was definitely becoming more social.

Back home, she set down her purse and called Ursula.

"I will see you there tomorrow morning at 10:00," Ursula replied. She hung up without asking if that time worked for JoLynne. The conversation was abrupt, as expected.

"Well," she said aloud. "At least I have a lesson scheduled. That was pretty brave if I do say so myself." She eyed her list, pinned to the refrigerator by a cruise ship magnet. She grabbed a pencil and added three more items, immediately crossing out the first two.

- Ride horses again

- Have sex

- Learn to swim

JoLynne stood back and admired her list. She was well on her way.

The next morning, she arrived at the pool to find Ursula already swimming laps. She slipped off her sweatshirt and shorts, placed them on a chair, and sat on the pool steps. She watched Ursula glide through the water, up and back, up and back, hardly making a splash but moving with speed and grace. There was so much more to this woman than JoLynne had ever assumed.

Eventually, Ursula stopped, spotted JoLynne, and asked, "Are you ready?"

"As I'll ever be," JoLynne replied.

"Wait for me!" called a voice from the library. Cass came through the door, shrugging out of a swimsuit cover-up and tossed her towel onto a lounge chair. "Ursula invited me," she said. "I hope that's okay."

"Hey, the more the merrier," said JoLynne. "You don't swim either?"

Cass shook her head. "When did I have time? I never learned. But it's stupid to live right by the ocean and not know how, don't you think?"

"Enough talking," said Ursula. "Put your face under the water and blow bubbles."

"I think any fool can do that," said JoLynne.

Cass muttered, "Then why am I nervous?"

Ursula did not laugh.

So JoLynne and Cass obediently put their faces under the water and blew bubbles. After a few minutes of that, Ursula handed them each a kickboard. "Go across the pool," she instructed.

"I don't know how," said JoLynne.

"You will figure it out," Ursula replied. "Put your forearms on the board. Stretch out. Kick as if your life depended on it."

With much splashing, struggle, and laughter, Cass and JoLynne made it across the pool. It helped that they were in the shallow end, which wasn't quite so scary. They came back under Ursula's watchful eye.

"Now," said Ursula, "put your face in the water. Stretch your arms out on the board. Kick gently. Stay afloat until you need a breath."

The lesson continued, with Ursula giving clear, simple instructions meant to build their confidence in the water. The pool was warm, and staying in the shallow end made things manageable. After an hour, JoLynne was feeling proud of herself. "Can we do this again soon?" she asked.

"I am available every Wednesday at this time," Ursula said.

"I'd like to pay you," said JoLynne.

Cass nodded. "Heck, yeah."

"I don't require money," Ursula said, already heading for her towel.

Cass and JoLynne gave each other a high-five as they got out and dried off. The three of them dressed and gathered their things.

"What made you want to teach us?" Cass asked.

"I have seen coworkers drown," Ursula said plainly. "It was unnecessary."

"Coworkers?" JoLynne asked, intrigued. "What kind of work were you in?"

"Swimming," Ursula replied without irony.

"Well," said Cass, "if you won't let us pay you, then I insist you both come to my house tonight for happy hour. Gus is on the road, and I could use the company. Say, four-ish?"

JoLynne, mindful of her list, answered quickly. "Sounds good to me."

Ursula said nothing.

Cass looked at her. "Well? Are you coming?"

Ursula nodded once. Then she stood and left.

JoLynne and Cass watched her go. "She is one strange character," JoLynne said.

"I like her," said Cass. "She's tough. Do you know anything about her background? You've been here longer than I have."

JoLynne shook her head. "Not really. But we could try to find out tonight."

That evening, JoLynne grabbed a bottle of wine and climbed into her golf cart to drive over to Cass's house, not far away. Ursula was already there, parking her own cart.

"Thanks again for the lesson today," JoLynne said. "I feel like I got a real workout."

"Swimming is good for you," said Ursula. "It helps your mind and your body."

"Hey, you two," called Cass from the porch.

Music from a smooth jazz station drifted from inside, and the three women made their way out back to the patio. JoLynne noticed that there had been gardening done. Now that Cass didn't have to move out, she had definitely moved in. Her former house was rented to two elderly women as a vacation property, and she had wasted no time putting her stamp on Gus's place with color, plants, and cheer.

"You've really started changing things around," said JoLynne.

Cass grinned. "He needed it. And he likes it."

They sat down at the patio table. Wind chimes jingled in the distance. A soft breeze swept through. It was summer, and Serena Cove buzzed with the sounds of vacationers. JoLynne had lived in the park for several years before Gene moved in and she became his caregiver. But it was only now, after his passing, that she was beginning to feel like she actually lived here. And with her list of goals, she felt like she was starting an entirely new chapter in the second half of her life. She sipped her wine, content. "Are you ever going to tell us what you used to do?" she asked Ursula. "Leonard says you were an Olympic swimmer."

Ursula shook her head. "I swam when I was in what you would call high school. But that ended because I had to go to work to support my family. I became a secretary for an East German company. I had many American acquaintances."

JoLynne leaned closer. "What kind of company?"

"I did some work for the American government," said Ursula. "Then, when the Wall fell, I continued that work, ostensibly as a secretary."

"Ooh, that sounds exciting," said Cass. "Were you like... a spy?"

Ursula shrugged. "I was simply a secretary. I was sent to various locations around the world. I observed. I reported."

Cass blinked. "I don't understand."

"I do," said JoLynne. "Thank you for your service to our country."

Ursula looked over at her. "A few years ago, I would have told you to stop being so dramatic. But now, it reminds me that I miss it. In comparison, the park is a very quiet place to live."

"I like that aspect," said JoLynne.

"I am trying." Ursula sipped her wine.

"Is that where you met the man we sometimes see you with?" Cass asked.

"Amir," said Ursula. "He and I worked together. We enjoyed each other's company." She paused, eyes growing distant. "We promised each other that, once we were no longer bound to employers, we'd return to some of these places as tourists. And now he wants me to join him in Istanbul."

"That sounds incredible," said Cass. "I'd go in a heartbeat."

"How do you feel about it?" JoLynne asked.

"I don't know if I can learn how to have this man in my life," Ursula said. "Not in that way. Not now."

"But you care about each other," said Cass. "At the very least, you're longtime friends."

"That is true," said Ursula. "But I have my life here now." She didn't look happy.

JoLynne sipped her wine, then set it down. "I am trying to break out of my old ways and try something new. I'm not downshifting. I'm gearing up."

Ursula looked at her. "We are the same age, yes?"

"I'm sixty-three," said JoLynne.

"I am sixty-five," said Ursula. "But I feel as though I have already lived my life."

"We're too young to say that," said Cass.

JoLynne gave her a look. "You're twenty years younger than us. You sure you belong here?"

Cass got mooney-eyed. "I belong wherever Gus is."

Ursula nodded. "The truck driver needed someone. I think you are good for him." She turned to JoLynne. "And you. I think you should let the rancher in."

JoLynne narrowed her eyes. "How do you know about the rancher?"

Ursula gave her a hard look. "Do you really have to ask me that question?"

"Hey," said Cass, "did you guys see Chuck flirting with Diane?"

The three of them launched into a discussion of the oddball pairing. JoLynne looked around the table at her friends. This was what she had wanted when she moved to Serena Cove: friends, laughter, and happy hour on a patio, with the sound of surf crashing in the distance.

She'd done right by Gene. Now it was her time, and for the first time in years, she felt ready for what came next.

Thirteen

JoLynne parked her truck near the barn and stepped out into the crisp mid-morning quiet. There was the hush familiar on rural land, broken only by the occasional whinny, the scuff of a hoof, the low creak of barn wood adjusting in the sun. The horses stood along the fence line, heads lifting at her approach, ears swiveling. She greeted each by name, her palm smoothing down warm velvet muzzles before she slipped into the tack room.

Letting herself into the barn, she studied the setup, how everything had a place. It looked lived-in, practical. The smell of oiled leather and sweet feed hit her all at once, and before she'd even finished scanning the shelves, her fingers were already reaching for a stiff-bristled brush and an old towel. Her hands moved with a memory that took her back to childhood.

By mid-morning, she'd groomed both big horses and was ready to brush Hashtag, the pony, who was hamming it up like a sucker for attention. He kept nipping at her blouse and then tossing his head up and down as if laughing at his own cleverness. The first time, JoLynne reprimanded him, but then when he kept it up, she found a flattened soccer ball and gave it to him to play with. Hashtag grasped it in his teeth and trotted around the corral. With his small stature and rounded belly, he definitely had some Shetland in him. When he stopped in front of her, she pulled gently on his forelock.

"Well, aren't you just a little showboat," she murmured, scratching behind his ears.

He turned his head like a dog and leaned into her hand. All the pony wanted was to have someone pay attention to him.

She grabbed a brush and began to work her way down the pony's coat. Her muscles remembered the rhythm of the brush stroke, the weight of the bucket, the stretch of her back when she leaned into the job. She was happy to be back on a ranch, around the sounds and smells of horses. Horses were her first love, with their beautiful galloping bodies and liquid eyes.

Working around them, she felt strong and unburdened. No appointments to schedule, no medications to track, no surly husband sighing behind her in a chair. Just a horse, a breeze, and the sun warming her shoulders.

It was too bad that Beau had so much on his plate that taking care of three horses was too much. She wondered why he even had three. It was more than they needed. Horses should always be a pleasure, not a duty.

She took a break to sip from her water bottle, wiping the sweat from her brow. He wouldn't like that she was there, but JoLynne had decided to take the reins. He needed help, and she needed horses. She capped the water bottle, a faint tightness blooming beneath her right ribs. It was sharper than a cramp but gone as soon as she noticed it. Probably all the unfamiliar activity. Still, she made a mental note to drink more water. It wouldn't be good to become dehydrated.

After she got done brushing Hashtag, she kissed him on his forehead and slipped through the fence.

"You be good," she said.

The pony followed her along the fence line, nickering softly, not willing to give up her companionship. But there was more to do and time was passing quickly. Once Hashtag looped around the back of the barn and into the paddock leading to his stall, she fastened the gate shut so she could ride the other horses around in the corral. She didn't feel quite bold enough to ride alone down the trail to the creek, not without Beau around. There were too many unknowns, and she respected how quickly a situation with horses could change.

Instead, she saddled Shorty, the gentlest of the three, and walked her into the corral. The other two watched, pacing in and out of their paddocks as if mildly offended they weren't also chosen.

Inside the corral, JoLynne led Shorty over to a mounting block and stuck her foot into the stirrup. In a pinch, she had no problem getting up into the saddle, but she wasn't that limber anymore, and the thoroughbred was gigantic. She clucked at the horse and rode slow circles at first, loosening up both the mare and her own body, which had forgotten some of the small muscles it used to know by heart.

It wasn't like the horse was getting a good workout, but it kept her moving, kept her joints from stiffening, and reminded her how she was supposed to behave when under saddle. If a horse went too long without being ridden, it could become pasture-sour and resist the bit and saddle.

JoLynne was happy to help because it was good to be up on a horse again, and it was something Beau wouldn't have to do later. She rode in circles around the corral, which was boring but peaceful. Then she'd turn Shorty around and have her circle the other way. After a half-hour of back and forth, round and round, trotting and walking, JoLynne dismounted. She removed Shorty's tack, returned her to the stall, and gave her some grain while she brushed her.

Across the barn aisle, Buck was craning his neck, waiting for his turn. A little while later, JoLynne repeated the endeavor with him. As she circled the corral, a breeze came up, cooling her skin and filling her with gratitude. For the first time in a long time, she felt like she'd come home to her real, natural life. How many years had it been! This was the true JoLynne:

aboard a horse, the breeze in her face, the sounds and smells of a ranch in her nostrils. Though she lived almost an hour away, this had to be a new routine for her. She had the time, and Beau needed the help. She hoped he wouldn't be mad when he got home and found out she'd been there.

After Buck was turned out and the tack put away, JoLynne headed over to the main house to see if Nate could give her another couple of bottles of water. She knocked on the door and waited, arms crossed, wondering what she'd find. Or whom.

A moment later, the door creaked open. Nate stood there in a stained T-shirt, a mug of coffee in one hand, as if he'd just woken up even though it was midafternoon.

"Hey, Nate," she said. "I'm JoLynne? From the other day?"

"I remember you," Nate muttered. "Beau's at work."

"I know that. I was just working the horses, and I'm parched. Can I get a drink of water?"

"You were out there working? I didn't know." He stepped back, holding the door open. "Come on in."

JoLynne stepped over the threshold, hesitating a moment as her eyes adjusted to the dimmer light inside. The house smelled like old books and metal solvent. The living room spilled directly into the kitchen, with no clear border between the spaces. A narrow couch sat sunken and slouched against the far wall, covered in a faded red wool blanket. Stacks of unopened mail and repairs in progress claimed the surfaces: a disassembled toaster on the counter, a battery tester on the dining table, a screwdriver sitting on a dinner plate.

She stood quietly, taking in the clutter, the weight of family history.

"I'd like to sit for a minute, if you wouldn't mind," she said, a sharp stitch flaring again under her ribs. She kept her face neutral.

Nate slid a chair out from the table. "You look a little flushed. Too much sun?"

"I'm fine. Just some water would be good."

"Coming up." Despite his limp and worn-down posture, there was something courtly in the way he spoke. He pulled a cold bottle from the fridge and cracked the cap before handing it over. Then he sat down with a wince, both hands braced on his knees as he lowered himself into the chair across from her.

She took a couple of sips. Outside the screen door, a lone chicken scratched and pecked along the edge of the porch, bobbing its head with comic dignity. A breeze stirred the faded lace curtain above the sink, carrying in the scent of horses and dust.

JoLynne glanced at Nate again. In the angled light, he reminded her of one of her uncles back home, one of the tired ones who'd waited too long to move to town for a more comfortable life.

"This place could be something," she said, nodding toward the overgrown kitchen garden visible through the window. "It just looks like it needs a little work, but not much."

"Beau can't do more than he's doing," Nate replied.

"Why do you lean on him so much?" she asked.

"You're pretty blunt, aren't you?"

She capped her water. "It saves time."

Nate smirked, but then he rubbed his face as if exhausted. "I don't like it either. But it keeps him upright. The work. He needs to feel like he's the one holding it together."

"Don't you think that's taking advantage of him?"

"My brother's a draft horse. If he's not pulling, he's not happy."

"Then I guess you two are perfect for each other," JoLynne said flatly.

Nate just sat there as if he hadn't heard.

"Thank you for the water." She stood, brushed off her jeans. Her side ached again, quick and sharp, then gone. She'd probably done too much and would rest when she got home.

"Thanks for helping with the horses." Nate walked her to the door. "You sure you feel all right?"

"I'm fine." She exhaled through her nose and walked back toward her car, the pony nickering as she walked past. She was just climbing into her SUV when movement in her rearview caught her attention.

Beau's truck was pulling in behind her.

Fourteen

Beau surfaced from sleep slowly, the comfort of shared warmth lulling him for a moment. And then he remembered. JoLynne was there with him, and he smiled, half-asleep, feeling happy.

Although at first, he'd been mad. Stopped what he was doing right there on the warehouse floor, in the middle of forklifts and pallets, rolling his eyes at the ceiling as he tried to process the information. Beau couldn't believe what his brother was telling him.

"JoLynne's at the house?"

"That's what I'm saying. Are you deaf?" Nate had called him at work to ask what his girlfriend was doing riding the horses out in the corral.

Beau hung up before he could say more. For a few minutes he just stood there, surrounded by his people and equipment, stepping aside to let a motorized pallet jack come through. He tried to make sense of it. She'd come all the way out to the ranch without telling him just so she could help with his chores.

By the time he'd made the turn off the highway, his anger had started to peel back, exposing something else underneath—shame, maybe. Guilt. Like he'd failed some unspoken test by needing her help at all. But beneath that, quieter and harder to admit, was gratitude. And a fear that she'd finish up and leave before he could see her.

Luckily, he'd arrived in time, and she'd hung around when he insisted on making her dinner. And then her head drooped and he put her to bed early, tucking her in wearing one of his old tee shirts.

Now, in the darkness of predawn, Beau reached for her, but the other side of the bed was cold. He blinked toward the window. It was still dark outside, but a faint gray light edged the horizon. From down the hallway, a narrow seam of light spilled under the bedroom door.

He stood, pulling on yesterday's jeans and padding barefoot into the hall. To his relief, the house smelled faintly of coffee, so she hadn't left. She'd probably risen early to make a pot and would be at the table with a mug in hand, reading something on her phone. That made him smile.

Then he turned the corner into the kitchen and saw her hunched over the counter. She wasn't sipping coffee. She wasn't moving at all.

"JoLynne?" He hurried to her side and put his hand on her back.

She jerked slightly at his touch, then stilled again.

"Hey, what's going on here? Are you sick?"

She didn't look at him. Just nodded once, eyes trained on the tile, one arm wrapped around her midsection. Her other hand braced against the edge of the sink. "I thought it was indigestion," she said quietly. "Or something like that. It woke me up." Her voice was thready, and she was frowning in pain.

Beau rubbed her back gently. "Did you find anything to take for it?"

"Antacids about an hour ago. It didn't help." She glanced up briefly, eyes rimmed with fatigue. "And there's a sharp pain right here." She tapped the lower right side of her rib cage, wincing slightly. "Kind of constant, like it's gripping me."

"Are you dizzy?" He felt her forehead. She was sweating.

"No dizziness," she said. "Just queasy. I looked it up. It might be my gallbladder. I've had it before, but not like this." She pushed her hair back, lips pressed tight. "It comes and goes sometimes after rich food, but this is new."

He reached toward the cabinet and got her a glass of water without asking. "Why didn't you wake me up?"

"I didn't want to overreact."

"You should have," he said. "You don't look so good."

That got him a faint smile. "I don't feel so good."

He stood in silence for a second, weighing what to do. "We should go to the ER."

JoLynne started to shake her head, then stopped. "I was thinking of texting Teresa, but it's so early."

"Text her. Or let me do it."

She pulled her phone from the counter and looked down at it, blinking against the light. "You do it. I can't think straight."

Beau took the phone gently, already scrolling for Teresa's number. He stepped away just enough to read the screen as he composed the message.

JoLynne's got pain in her right side, nausea, antacids didn't help. Thinking gallbladder. What would you do?

He hit send and glanced back at her. She was still leaning against the counter, breathing slow and steady through her nose.

"Come sit," he said, helping her into a chair. "Want me to call Teresa?"

"Let's just wait. She gets up early. She might text back."

The overhead light was too bright, so he turned it off, leaving only the lamp over the stove. JoLynne managed a sip of water, then another. She didn't talk, and he didn't push. He sat nearby, waiting quietly with her. Whatever this was, it had knocked her flat, and he didn't want to crowd her, but he wasn't leaving her alone, either.

Her phone buzzed. Teresa's reply was blunt and immediate.

If it's radiating into your shoulder, don't mess around. Go now.

JoLynne stared at it, puffing out a breath. "I was hoping for something a little less scary."

"Do you feel pain radiating?" Beau's anxiety dialed up a notch. He didn't even know what the hell a gallbladder did, but "pain radiating" sounded bad.

She nodded. "Into my back and shoulder, yeah."

Beau reached past her and took the phone, not asking. "I'll grab your bag and get your shoes."

He kneeled in front of her and helped slip them on. Then he stood, her purse over his shoulder, keys in hand.

"I hate this," she said, letting him help her up. "I hate hospitals."

"Me too," he said, "but I'd rather take you in and find out it's nothing, than stay here and realize it's serious."

He held the door open, and they stepped out into the dark. The air was cool, the gravel under their feet loud in the quiet morning. Stars still shimmered over the hills, but the sky was beginning to turn gray at the edges.

Beau helped her up into the truck. She settled in slowly, one hand still pressed to her side. He reached across her and fastened her seatbelt gently.

The truck rolled out of the gravel drive and onto the empty road, headlights catching the low fog along the shoulders. Beau kept one hand on the wheel and the other resting on the console, fingers twitching like they wanted to do more. But there wasn't much he could do right now, and that was hard for him.

JoLynne leaned her head back against the seat, eyes half-closed. She wasn't groaning or gasping. Although she didn't complain, she kept her hand tight over her side, and every now and then she'd shift, like she couldn't get comfortable.

"You cold?" he asked, glancing at her.

"No."

"Do you want the radio on quiet?"

"Just drive. Please?

He nodded. The road was mostly empty this time of night. One delivery truck passed them going the other direction, but that was it. For a while, there was only the hum of the tires and the soft rasp of her breathing.

Then, out of nowhere, she said, "So much for making your life easier."

Beau glanced at her. She had one eyebrow raised, just barely, the ghost of a smile on her lips. He gently rubbed the back of her neck before returning to the job of driving.

They passed the turnoff to an old diner. Beau's headlights lit up the "Closed" sign in the window.

JoLynne cleared her throat. "Thanks for not freaking out."

"It wouldn't have helped."

"No." She paused. "You're steady. It's a comfort."

He wanted to be that for her. He tightened his grip on the wheel and kept driving.

Ramona was only a few minutes away now. The first signs of town were appearing, with dark storefronts, empty gas stations, and a blinking yellow caution light at the crossroads.

"Almost there," he said.

At the hospital, the automatic doors of the emergency room sighed open as Beau guided her inside, holding her with one arm. The waiting room was nearly empty, with a woman holding a sleeping child on her lap and an older man staring at the news station on the television up on the wall. The fluorescent lights made everything look bleached out and tired. JoLynne blinked against the glare as they approached the triage desk.

"Symptoms?" the nurse asked, tapping keys.

"Abdominal pain on my right side," JoLynne said, quietly but clearly. "I have nausea and I feel feverish. I took antacids, but it didn't help."

The nurse glanced up, nodding as she typed. "Pain radiating anywhere?"

JoLynne rolled her head, wincing. "In my back, near my shoulder blade."

"History of this before?"

"No. Just twinges sometimes after heavy food. Nothing like this."

The nurse handed her a clipboard. "Fill this out. We'll get you back as soon as we can."

JoLynne sat gingerly, Beau beside her, watching her out of the corner of his eye. She filled out the form slowly, pausing every few lines to catch her breath. Her handwriting was neat, deliberate. No one would know she was in pain unless they looked closely.

A nurse called her name ten minutes later. Beau hesitated, but JoLynne nodded. "I'm okay. Go park the truck."

"I'll be here as long as it takes."

She followed the nurse through the swinging doors, her body listing to one side. Beau watched her go, feeling useless. If there were a way to carry it for her, he would have.

The exam room was small, curtained off from the others. JoLynne slipped into the gown and lay on the gurney, squinting against the harsh light. An IV was started, and she shut her eyes against all the usual annoyances. The nurse asked her more questions about her pain level, allergies, and time of last meal. JoLynne gave clipped answers, her jaw clenched. She hated the way her voice sounded. Thin, and a little pathetic.

The ultrasound tech came and went. Her IV bag hung cold beside her bed. The curtain rustled every now and then when someone walked past.

JoLynne hated this kind of waiting. She'd spent too many years sitting by hospital beds, chasing after information, begging nurses to get a doctor to come to Gene's room where she waited. Only this time, she was the one in the bed, and there was nothing she could do but lie still and wait for some stranger to come in and rule on her life.

The nurse appeared again. "Do you have someone to take you home after surgery?"

JoLynne lifted her head. "Am I having surgery?"

The nurse offered a polite half-smile. "I'll let the doctor discuss that with you."

Resigned to whatever was going to happen, JoLynne laid back. "My friend is in the waiting room. Can you get him?"

Moments later, she heard Beau's voice at the end of her bed. "How're you doing?"

Just then, the doctor arrived wearing dark blue scrubs and a stethoscope looped around her neck. She was maybe mid-thirties, South Asian, with steady eyes, her dark hair clipped into a no-nonsense bun. She introduced herself, described the reasons gallbladder removal was necessary, and soon. Then she patted JoLynne on the arm and whooshed away through the curtains.

Once the doctor had left, silence settled between them. Beau sat in the hard plastic chair. "Looks like they're going to get right on it," he said. "I'll be here when you're out."

"Thanks, but you should go home. You've got the horses—"

"JoLynne." His mouth formed a straight line. "I said I'll be here."

Closing her eyes, she nodded.

They settled in for the wait. Somewhere outside, a cart rolled by with a metallic clatter. A monitor beeped steadily behind her, syncing up with the drip-drip-drip of the IV in her arm. JoLynne heard Beau shift in the chair beside her, the creak of the plastic and metal always the sound of hospitals and waiting.

"Do you want me to call someone for you?" he asked, breaking the silence. "Vivian, maybe?"

"Teresa," JoLynne murmured, eyes still closed. "Text her an update."

Beau reached for her phone where it sat near her hand on the bed. "I'll call her." He stood and stepped just outside the curtain.

JoLynne opened one eye, saw that he was gone, and closed it again. The lights overhead beat through her eyelids. You'd think the hospital would at least give you a hand towel or something to block the glare.

When Beau returned, he sat down and handed her phone back. "Teresa said to keep her posted, and that she can help once you get home."

"I hate to bother her," said JoLynne. She couldn't believe she was in this situation. Being single and older, of course it had occurred to her to wonder what she would do if it ever arose. But like most people, she had shoved the prospect to the back of her mind. No reason to borrow trouble, as her mother used to say.

A moment later, the nurse appeared with consent forms and a clipboard. Beau stood quietly while JoLynne signed them. When the nurse left again, JoLynne spoke, her voice soft. "This wasn't supposed to happen today."

"Nope," Beau said.

"I hate having people fuss over me."

"Nobody's fussing," he said. "We're waiting together, and then I'm going to take you home when you get out."

She turned her head slightly toward him. "Jesus, Beau. We hardly know each other."

Beau laughed out loud. "That's changin' real fast, isn't it?"

A different nurse came in, explaining they were going to prep her for surgery, and put something into her IV. The medication slid into her veins with an odd coldness, followed by a soft, floaty warmth. Her eyelids felt heavier. Her thoughts slowed. Then came the quiet shuffle of wheels and shoes and a man's voice, gentle and efficient.

She felt Beau give her hand a warm squeeze before they wheeled her away.

Fifteen

V ivian came through JoLynne's bedroom door, eyes wide. "There's a
Chippendale dancer out back doing yardwork with his shirt off."

JoLynne gave a sleepy smile. Her eyes were still so heavy, and in the
several days since she'd left the hospital, she'd hardly got out of bed.

Thank God for Beau. He'd waited for her to get out of surgery, taken her
home, and stayed at her house ever since. He slept in her king-size bed with
her, but they only cuddled. JoLynne always had a hard time recovering
from anesthesia.

"That's Beau," she mumbled to Vivian. "My boyfriend, I think."

"Either that or a spectacular-looking gardener." Vivian dragged the
kitchen chair closer to the bed, unwound her scarf, and sat down. Leaning
close, she rested her hand on JoLynne's forehead for a moment. "You're
nice and cool," she said.

"Yeah, I'm better," said JoLynne, opening her eyes. "I have to say, this
has thrown me for a loop." It wasn't just the surgery that threw her. It was
Beau, too, being here, taking care of her.

"You don't like having a good-lookin' man waiting on you hand and foot? What the hell is wrong with you?" Vivian grinned. "Honey, you know what they say. Lie back and enjoy it."

JoLynne gave her sister a wry smile. The woman was incorrigible.

"Help me sit up." Once she was comfortable, she spotted Vivian's overnight case by the door. "Are you sticking around?"

"That was the plan. I thought you were on death's door, the way you sounded on the phone, but I can see you don't need me at all."

"You can stay," said JoLynne. She always enjoyed having her sister around.

"Not if I have a choice between that pullout and a real bed," said Vivian.

"I'm sorry." The spare bedroom was still cluttered with Gene's things.

"Don't worry about it," said Vivian. "I'll just book a room in La Jolla. That place I like, with the spa."

Vivian did like her spa treatments. And she could afford them.

"So, tell me everything about Chip out there."

"Beau," said JoLynne.

"Fine, whatever. Just spill it." Vivian made a gimme gesture, and JoLynne began to talk.

"He's just so good," she said, feeling herself glow as she spoke of riding horses at his ranch, and how much he cared about it and his brother. How hard he worked taking care of everybody. And how good-natured and practical he was.

"You like him a lot."

"I do," JoLynne said, the wonder of it hitting her all at once. She ran her hand through her unwashed hair. "He'll be coming in to make lunch pretty soon. Do you think you could help me get presentable?"

"I'll get the water runnin'," said Vivian.

Lunch was fun. With her sister's help, JoLynne had blow-dried her hair, and she felt like a new woman. The two of them kept cracking her up.

Vivian with her big laugh, and Beau with his dry country humor, until JoLynne had to beg them to stop before she popped a stitch.

After Viv left, Beau got the sofa ready, arranging pillows and a blanket. When she stood too fast and got dizzy, he was instantly at her side, his arm slipping around her waist.

"Can you make it to the couch?" he asked, worry lines creasing his brow.

JoLynne was embarrassed and frustrated by how weak and needy she felt.

"That's how it goes," said Beau. "Next time it's me facedown, you pull me up. Okay?"

"Okay," she said, easing down on the couch.

As soon as she was settled, Beau returned to the kitchen to clean up. She watched him maneuvering around, putting things in the dishwasher, wiping down the counters. She felt grateful. And safe.

He made it easy to accept help, and that wasn't her normal comfort zone. From the moment he brought her home from the hospital, it'd been one humiliation after the next, from helping her to the restroom to the mortification of post-surgical gas pains.

Beau joked gently, "Just blame it on the dog."

"I don't have a dog." She threw a pillow at him.

While she dozed lightly, Beau replaced a broken hinge on a dish cabinet. He cleaned her coffee maker. He tightened the screws on her wobbly kitchen table.

Sleepy, JoLynne watched him in wonder. "Do you ever stop?"

"I like to work with my hands."

He made a face at something, and she caught it.

"Some things in here really do need refurbishing," she said.

"Did you have a lot to do when you bought the place?"

"It was in pretty bad shape, but like you, I'm handy. Even though I've spent my life working behind a desk, I know my way around an electric saw and a drill. And there's all that information online to help you. I was making good progress... then Gene moved in." Her voice trailed off.

"It's hard when you've got someone with a chronic illness," said Beau.

JoLynne rubbed her forehead. "He started going downhill fast, right as soon as he moved in. And then he hung on for a few years. I didn't have anything left over for this place. If a hinge fell off, I used duct tape. If a light died, I used another lamp. You get used to working around it."

Beau perched on the arm of the couch. "Darlin', you don't have to worry about that now. Not while I'm here."

"How are you even finding the time?" she asked. "Who's doing the feeding?"

He leaned down and brushed a strand of hair from her forehead. "Nate can handle it if it's just for a few days. Feeding's simple, mostly. And if he misses something, I can swing by, check things. No big deal."

JoLynne raised an eyebrow. Beau giving up control? That didn't quite square with the man she was coming to know. "You'd let him take over?"

Beau hesitated. "For short periods, he's okay. He can do the work. He just gets overwhelmed easy. If too many things hit at once, he... kinda freezes up. It's easier if I stay ahead of it."

JoLynne nodded slowly. Something in his tone made her glance at him a little longer. A half-formed question rose in her mind, not about the ranch, exactly, but about how Beau managed to carry so much, but she let it pass.

"Anyway," he said, "it's nice not having to commute back and forth to Ramona. Saves me a ton of time and energy, so stop worrying. You're actually helping me out."

"If you say so," she said.

The doorbell rang. He gave her hand a squeeze and stood up. "It's that German woman. You feel like company?"

"Why not?"

She heard the door open, then Beau's voice, polite and easy. "Come on in."

"Here is soup," said Ursula in her usual, icy tone.

Then Cass's laugh floated in, quick and warm.

JoLynne smiled to herself, waiting. She wondered what her friends were thinking, seeing Beau in all his tall and handsome glory, with that clean T-shirt snug across his chest.

By the time the two women came around the corner, Cass was grinning, and Beau was carrying Tupperware. "It's lentil soup," he said.

Ursula nodded. "High protein. Easy on the system."

"This is really nice of you," said JoLynne, genuinely touched.

Cass flopped into the armchair and handed over a six-pack of something with bright labels and foreign script. "Drink one of these. It's supposed to be good for your immune system."

JoLynne squinted at the bottle. "Blood orange and cardamom?"

"It's healthy. Want one?" She held out a bottle to Ursula, who shivered dramatically and shook her head. Cass cracked one open for herself.

Beau stuck the soup in the fridge. "I'll be outside if you ladies need anything."

After closing the sliding glass door behind him, the women watched Beau walk away.

"Ranch life agrees with him," said Ursula.

"No kidding," said Cass. "So, he's here helping you? Like, staying with you?" She raised her eyebrows.

"I couldn't be alone, so he stepped up," said JoLynne. "It's just weird, though. I mean really, we haven't known each other that long. It's a lot, him being here." She sighed, remembering Gene. "I don't like thinking I might be a burden."

"It's temporary," Cass said. "You'll be back to normal in another day or two."

Ursula nodded. "You're healing. It's a process."

They settled in around her like old friends, gossiping and laughing. JoLynne shifted against her pillows, still sore, but buoyed by the company.

Beau, Vivian, Cass, Ursula, and Teresa were all concerned about her. If it took a medical emergency to bring people together, well, it was a nice silver lining.

After seeing JoLynne, Ursula returned home and stood in the middle of her spotless living room, uncertain what to do with herself. The silence pressed in.

She moved to fluff a pillow, then straightened a tchotchke, brushing a speck of dust from the brass Eiffel Tower from the last time they'd been in Paris. Those were good times.

The agency had sent Amir to investigate a shipment of weapons headed for the Middle East, and in an uncharacteristically impulsive moment, Ursula had followed him, surprising him at a café with her hair down in waves and nothing on under a black coatdress. He'd sat across from her, his eyebrows raised at the thought of her depravity. Then he'd waved his hand impatiently to flag the waiter for the check. They'd hurried out of the café, down the sidewalk, up a flight of stairs. One hand around her waist, one on the key, he unlocked the door, drew her inside, and pressed her against the wall, covering her with kisses until her knees sagged. Then he picked her up and carried her to his bed.

Ursula caught her breath, remembering. In those days, he was a lion.

For the next few days, they rarely left his tiny apartment overlooking the Seine except to eat and restore themselves. When his work was done, they traveled. Canal boats, bike riding through the countryside, and picnics on the grounds of crumbling castles. They spent two weeks living as if they were a couple, without a single care for the future or past.

High on lust and international intrigue, Ursula had never felt more powerful. When she was strong, Amir met her strength with his own. When he was vulnerable, she was kind. It was the most tender and glorious time of her life.

Now, her shoulders slumped. She was old. Those years were behind her.

Grow up, she thought, scowling at herself.

Serena Cove had been a choice. She could have lived anywhere in the world, but she chose this small, forgotten, shabby mobile home park on the edge of the Pacific Ocean for its anonymity and limitless blue horizon.

Being at JoLynne's house, chatting with the women, making an attempt to integrate herself, that was good, too. Appropriate for this time in her life.

Soon, she would qualify for a state pension, though she didn't need it, having lived carefully and invested wisely.

Still, she was restless.

She thought again about Amir's invitation. A month in Istanbul.

But he was unrealistic, his head full of passion. They needed to accept that their time had passed.

Ursula considered throwing the figurine in the wastebasket, but instead she slipped it into the cherry wood hutch where it couldn't be seen.

She needed to let him go. Let him run.

Tonight, she would give him the answer she should've sent a year ago.

Sixteen

A beach ball rolled toward JoLynne and Beau, blowing across the damp sand and heading for the water. Before the waves could snatch it, Beau trotted forward and kicked it gently back toward the children sprinting after it.

"Thank you!" A boy of about eight grabbed the ball and waved enthusiastically before tearing off again.

He was so cute and earnest that JoLynne laughed. "That was very gallant of you."

"I try," Beau said, slipping his hand into hers.

The walk had been her idea, since she was feeling better and needed to stretch her legs. As usual, with Beau's helpfulness, the outing had escalated. Beach chairs, an umbrella, and a cooler stocked with snacks and drinks were now staged at their picnic site.

"Are you sure this isn't too much?" he asked.

"I'm fine." JoLynne smiled up at him. "Tell you the truth, I don't even feel like I had surgery."

A wave crashed closer than expected, and they stepped back, laughing, though not before the icy water washed over their bare feet.

"Oh my god," JoLynne said. "It's beautiful, but I will never get used to this cold."

"Yes, you will," Beau said. "Are you going to go back to your swimming lessons?"

"If Ursula is willing to keep teaching us." The woman had seemed restless lately. Preoccupied. Something was going on in that complicated head of hers, JoLynne felt certain. "Anyway, I'd much rather be flailing around in a pool than in the ocean. Beaches are for sitting on."

Beau stopped walking and gently turned her to face him. "But we had fun out there, didn't we?"

She pressed close, remembering his arms steady around her as the surf had surged in. "We always do, Beau."

He lowered his mouth to hers and kissed her right there on the beach, in the middle of a Saturday afternoon, with children shouting nearby and the sound of the ocean filling the air.

JoLynne smiled against his lips.

"What?" he asked, pulling back just enough to look at her.

"This," she said. "All of it."

"You're happy."

"How could you tell?" She kissed him again, then turned to continue their stroll up the beach, still holding his hand. They walked easily together, pointing out a windsurfer skimming across the water, a fishing vessel idling offshore, and far in the distance, a cruise ship heading south to Mexico.

JoLynne sighed. If a person had to have surgery, it probably wasn't ideal timing to do it at the very beginning of a relationship. And yet, what she had found in the aftermath felt unexpectedly golden. She and Beau had grown close over the past couple of weeks, enjoying meals together, quiet evenings on the patio, and reading side by side on the couch. With Beau, she felt a kind of intimacy that was gentle and unforced.

But sometimes she'd look up and catch him worrying, and it weighed on her.

Every few days, Nate called with some issue at the ranch. Beau never complained, but she could see the tension in his face, in his posture. More than once, he had gone straight to the ranch after work, only to show up at her house later at night, just before she went to bed.

"You don't have to run yourself ragged like this," she had told him.

"I feel better knowing you're not alone at night."

"But I'm healing great."

"I know," he'd said. "I'll go home eventually. Just humor me for now."

She had agreed, understanding that this was how he showed he cared, with service and presence. By showing up. And it was working. For the first time in years, JoLynne was beginning to believe she could trust herself again. That a couple of bad decisions earlier in her life might not mean she was incapable of choosing.

Beau was a good guy. She would enjoy him while she could, miss him when he wasn't around, and hope he figured out an easier way of life before he keeled over from a heart attack.

They reached their spot and settled into their folding chairs. Beau stared out at the water, his expression distant.

She reached into the cooler, handed him a beer, and took one for herself. "What's bothering you?"

"You can read me pretty well," he said.

"I pay attention."

He tapped his can lightly against hers, took a sip, then set it in the chair's holder. He rubbed his palm against his knee, brushing sand that wasn't there. "I think it's probably time for me to head back to the ranch," he said. "As much as I hate to."

"I know," she said. "It's not like you live here, even though it's felt like it for a while."

"And it was really nice." He reached for her hand.

They sat without speaking, watching clouds build along the horizon.

"I'm worried about something Nate mentioned about the barn," Beau continued. "The wiring. That kind of thing falls on me. I should be there. I keep thinking I'll get him to step up one of these days. Until he does, I'm pretty much stuck. I don't want anything bad to happen to him or the ranch."

"Hey," JoLynne said. "I get it. I have siblings. Well, a sibling." She looked down at her beer, where drops of condensation ran down the icy sides.

"What's wrong?" Beau asked.

She let out a small, humorless breath. "I guess you can see me pretty well, too."

"I pay attention," he said. "Tell me."

"Okay, well, you've met Vivian."

"She's amazing."

"That's what I told her about you," JoLynne said. She stared out at the ocean, gathering herself. Then she cleared her throat.

"Vivian and I grew up on a ranch," she began.

And then the words started pouring out of her. "We had a little brother. Joshua. He was so cute. A little pest, but in a sweet way. I mean, I was a teenager, so I didn't think that at the time. I do now."

JoLynne swallowed. "Our dad was gruff and overworked, and my mom was kind but stretched thin. So Viv and I did a lot of the raising, even though it pissed us off. Sometimes we'd ditch him, but since there weren't any other kids to play with, we'd end up feeling sorry for him and go find him. Let him ride with us, help with the horses, that kind of thing."

Beau remained silent, waiting.

"I was at a barrel racing competition one day. I had just finished, and I was so excited! I won first place, and I got to stand on a riser and wave to the crowd while the announcer talked about my time. It was really neat." She closed her eyes. "My aunt was waiting for me when I came back out of the arena. She said we had to go home. Joshua had been hurt."

Beau's hand slid gently into hers.

"He was trying to imitate me, racing around the corral on Vivian's horse, which was too much for him," JoLynne said. "He got flung off and hit his head on a fence post. He never woke up. He was eight."

The two of them sat silently while the surf crashed onto the sand. A line of pelicans drafted each other over the water.

"Vivian never rode again. As for me, that day at the ranch, when you invited me and I met your friends? That was my first time riding since Joshua." She stared at the water, breathing carefully.

"Oh, man, I'm so sorry," said Beau.

"It's been fifty years!" she said, "and it still feels so hard sometimes. Mom and Dad never got over it. So when you say you can't abandon Nate, I get it." She blinked at him, her eyes brimming. "I do."

Beau gathered her into his arms and held her. She leaned into him, pressing her face against his chest and letting his warmth steady her.

When the ache eased, she straightened.

"Better?"

"Yeah." She swiped tears from her cheeks. "Thanks for listening."

"Thank you for telling me."

"So this is what I think," she said. "Your ranch is important, and so is Nate. You should go, and when you're ready to come back, I'll be waiting."

"You'd better be," he said, lifting her chin. Their kiss was tender and a little sad but also encouraging. They were in this together, thought JoLynne. They had each other's backs. Life didn't get easier, but maybe she didn't have to carry all of it alone.

She glanced at Beau. He felt her gaze. Turning to her, he gave her a solemn nod, as if he were thinking the same thing.

That night, Beau lay on his back in the dark, listening. The house creaked occasionally, soft sounds settling into quiet. He tilted his head slightly, watching the gentle rise and fall of the blankets. He could make out the faint shape of her profile, but her breathing was so quiet it made his chest tighten.

He reached a hand across the sheets, just resting it lightly against her hip, not to wake her, only to anchor himself.

This woman.

He'd thought coming here was temporary, a favor for someone he considered a friend. Someone who deserved better than what she'd got. But now, lying here in the quiet of midnight, he felt something he hadn't in years. Hope and the prospect of freedom.

It was so easy to imagine waking up next to her every morning, having breakfast with her before leaving for work. Fixing the broken bits of the house in slow, satisfying turns. Her laughter in the kitchen. Quiet evenings with nothing to worry about. Her house was small but sweet. He could help make it shine.

It was probably too much to hope for, but if he could get Nate squared away, maybe he'd look for a rental nearby. A little house or even an apartment over a garage. Something simple that would allow him to stay close and give whatever it was between them time to develop.

JoLynne had already told him he was welcome anytime, that he could stash a toothbrush and that she'd empty a dresser drawer for him. She meant it.

Beau told himself for the hundredth time that he wasn't going to worry about Gene's damn message anymore. The odds of her finding it were almost nonexistent. Gene's phone accounts had been shut down. Deleted. And even if something did resurface, hadn't Beau shown her who he really was? Hadn't he proved it, over and over, since the day she came home from the hospital? Still, some nights, the thought returned. A loose thread he couldn't quite pull free of.

Beau turned onto his side and looked at her sleeping form, quiet and trusting. God help him, he wasn't sure he deserved the peace he'd found here, with this kind woman, in this little house. But if he had to fight to keep it, he would.

Seventeen

Beau was at his desk with half a muffin in one hand and four browser tabs open—two with order forms, one with a spreadsheet, and one with an article about a replacement part he wasn't sure even existed anymore. His coffee sat cooling beside the monitor, mostly forgotten. Out on the floor below his mezzanine office, something heavy hit the concrete with a crash. He didn't flinch. It was just another Monday.

After saying goodbye to JoLynne yesterday, he'd driven back to the ranch with a lump in his throat and a to-do list already forming in his head. The barn was fine, but Hashtag's stall door was hanging crooked again, the drain in the lower trough was clogged with hay sludge, and a section of the pasture fence was bowing out like a herd of cattle had been leaning against it. All of it was fixable, and none of it was urgent, but it gnawed at him. Especially since the fence damage was in full view of the house. If Nate had been paying attention, he should've fixed it, or at least said something.

Beau hadn't said anything either. Instead, as he spent the weekend repairing everything by himself, moving from one chore to the next, he mustered his arguments. He didn't want a gigantic fight, but things had to change.

Now, back at the warehouse, his desk was a familiar mess covered with forms to sign, invoices to review, and a notice from the county that an inspection was required. Through the wide glass wall of his office, he spotted Darnell, one of the newer forklift guys, standing beside a pallet that was visibly listing to the left. Darnell was frozen, staring at the thing like it might fix itself. He glanced up, spotted Beau watching, and gave a sheepish little shrug.

Beau leaned toward the mic on the desk and pressed the intercom. "It's not going to straighten itself, Darnell." When the worker gave a thumbs-up, Beau clicked off the mic.

The door creaked open behind him. Selina stepped in, holding a tablet. She wore jeans, work boots, and a bright blue T-shirt with the company logo, her braid slung over one shoulder. She was young, in her mid-twenties, maybe. Smart and businesslike.

"Hey, boss," she said. "I have the revised inventory sheets you asked for. And FYI, Dock Three's still a mess. I think Paul got pulled away somewhere else."

"I didn't know that. Thanks." He studied the sheets for a minute while she waited. "Did you revise these?"

"Yeah, there was an upgrade available, so I applied it, and this is how it came out. Pretty cool, huh?"

"Very." Looking up at her, he gestured to the chair across from his desk. "Selina, you ever think about taking on more?"

She blinked. "All the time."

That made him smile. He sat down in his chair, the back creaking. "Something I'm wondering about. I could use help with the forklift rotation and staging layout. We're wasting square footage along the west wall. Maybe you've seen it."

"I have," she said. "If you want, I can sketch up a plan for organizing it better. Should I?"

"Thought you'd never ask," he said with a grin. "Let me know what you come up with."

She headed back out, already tapping something on her tablet. A few minutes later, she was down on the floor, flagging two guys and pointing to her screen. They nodded and got moving without a word.

And just like that, a problem that'd been weighing on him for weeks was on its way to being solved, and it turned out all he'd needed to do was ask. Sometimes he was such an idiot. Selina was solid, but she'd been underutilized.

He rubbed his chin. Where else might he be overlooking solutions that were staring him right in the face? Who else was waiting around to be given more responsibility?

Not that he hadn't trusted anyone before. He hired good people, and they delivered for him. But they could do more, grow more, if only their boss loosened the reins.

He let out a breath, spotting a note on the corkboard that had been there for three months. It read, "Fix dock lights." He had plenty of Selinas on staff. Maybe one of them worked in Maintenance. He should talk to the supervisor.

And it was definitely time to talk to Nate.

JoLynne drove her golf cart slowly toward the clubhouse, the breeze cool against her skin. Beau was gone. The house felt quiet without him, but she was far enough along in her healing to manage on her own, as long as she was careful.

Last night had been their farewell dinner. Beau barbecued ribs while she set the table and queued up some music. They kept the conversation light, avoiding the heavy topics they'd circled around for days. There was no fight, no final pronouncement. Just a gentle recognition that something was shifting.

That night, like every night since her surgery, they had snuggled under the covers, drifting off without making love. Even so, it was lovely. Reassuring. They had touched each other's faces, held each other's gaze, and felt the weight of the distance that was about to open up between them.

Until Beau figured out a better way to balance his life, she would have to step back and let him either continue to run himself ragged or find a new way forward. In the meantime, she would miss him, treasure the time they had shared, and keep working on her list.

That was one of the nice things about being in your sixties. You could hurt for someone without needing to fix them.

This morning, after a quiet breakfast, they kissed goodbye, both of them lingering, not quite ready to be the one to let go. Then he was gone.

Now, at the clubhouse, she unlocked the front door and walked through the entry, flipping on lights. It felt good to be upright and moving. She wandered through the common areas, dusted a bit here and there, straightened pillows and magazines, and tidied the kitchen counter. A few minutes later, Teresa arrived, arms full, a cardboard box clutched against her chest.

"We're having a free clinic today," she said.

"What do you need help with?" JoLynne stepped in quickly to support the box from underneath.

"Thanks. I'm going to set up in the library again. That door to the pool deck makes it easy for people to come straight in."

As they walked, Cass appeared at the gate and joined them, grabbing a second box from Teresa's car. The three of them carried supplies to the library and began unpacking. Teresa pointed to a portable blood pressure monitor, a few folders, and some pamphlets. "Sometimes I refer people out, but a lot of the time I can just help right here. One woman came in last month using a cane the wrong way, and I showed her how to position it opposite her weak leg. That one little adjustment made a huge difference."

Soon, Teresa had her table arranged, her forms stacked neatly, and her stethoscope slung around her neck. They sat together near the window, waiting for the first visitors to arrive.

"How are things with Beau?" Teresa asked.

JoLynne smiled softly. "Good. Complicated. He's back at the ranch now."

"Dan's buried in work too," Teresa said. "The firefighter training company is expanding to two more cities. He's thinking about hiring an assistant."

"No kidding?"

"Yeah. He keeps saying it'll get easier once he delegates, but I'll believe it when I see it."

The three of them waited, chatting between stretches of quiet. The longer they sat without visitors, the more discouraged Teresa looked.

"Maybe people forgot," said JoLynne.

"They'll come next time," Cass said. "These things take a while to catch on."

"You guys are sweet, but what I really need is a draw. Some kind of attraction."

"I'm not dressing up in a clown suit," said JoLynne. They laughed, but she was getting tired. "I'm going to check on Leonard and then head home."

"If you see him, ask him why the heck he's not here," growled Teresa.

JoLynne drove her cart to his house, knocked softly, and was greeted by a tall woman who looked to be in her early sixties, her silver hair falling in soft waves to her shoulders. A streak of blue coloring had been added, and it almost exactly matched her eyes.

"I'm here to see Leonard?" JoLynne said, wondering who the heck this was.

"He's expecting you." The woman held the screen open. "I'm his daughter, Vera."

"Nice to meet you." JoLynne walked past, trying to get a good look without being rude. Vera wore cute jeans with embroidered flowers from the knees to her bare feet. Her oversized knit top slouched off one shoulder, revealing a strap of blue tank top. She returned to the task of folding a pile of laundry on the dining room table.

JoLynne went into the living room where Leonard was sitting on the couch.

"Where's your recliner?" She pointed at the empty spot in the room.

Leonard and Vera exchanged a look. Then she hooked a thumb at him, smiling. "Go ahead, Dad. Fess up."

"We had to get rid of it," he admitted. "I dropped a bunch of food in it right through the hole in the seat. It was totaled."

"Ick," JoLynne said, scrunching her nose.

"That old thing's been on its last legs for years," said Vera. Her voice was raspy and quiet.

"She put it on the curb." Leonard looked repentant. "We'll have to find a replacement."

"I'll keep an eye out," said JoLynne. "And if you're not busy, Leonard, the nurse is doing health checks down at the clubhouse. She said for you to get your butt down there."

"Dad?" Vera looked at Leonard, who shrugged.

"Fine," he said. "But only if there aren't a bunch of nosy neighbors around."

"Nobody at all," said JoLynne, yawning. The morning had caught up with her. Her limbs felt heavy, and she leaned slightly.

"You just had surgery!" said Leonard. "And here we are, tiring you out."

"Do you need me to drive you home?" asked Vera.

"I'll be okay, but thanks." JoLynne said her goodbyes, walked back to her golf cart, and drove home. The house greeted her with stillness, which seemed sad, but she was too tired to think much about it. She kicked off her shoes, lay down on the bed, and closed her eyes. Sleep took her almost instantly.

In her dream, she was back at Beau's ranch. The air was sweet with hay and dust, the hills stretching gold and wide beneath a bright, endless sky. Somewhere nearby, laughter rang out, and then, the unmistakable clatter of hooves. Hashtag tore past her, tail flying, a stethoscope dangling from his teeth.

"Hey!" she called, breaking into a run, now with Teresa inexplicably running beside her in surgical scrubs. "Give that back!"

But the pony only tossed his head and picked up speed, running around in circles in the corral like it was all a game.

JoLynne woke up laughing at how ridiculous dreams could be. Still smiling, she swung her legs over the side of the bed. A ridiculous dream, and yet, maybe it was pointing her in the right direction. Teresa's clinic, but with a twist...

Eighteen

Driving up on the ranch's battered ATV, Beau spotted JoLynne standing near the barn, framed against the blue sky in a sun-creased Stetson and worn boots she'd won in her hometown rodeo. She stood with her hands on her hips, watching Hashtag tear around the pasture like a lunatic, an empty feed bucket clenched between his teeth.

She turned at the sound, already smiling.

Beau cut the engine and swung down. "Hey, beautiful." He folded her into an embrace, then drew back and lowered his mouth to hers. Her lips were so soft—

The feed bucket smacked against the fence. Hashtag stood there, nodding at them.

"That pony!" JoLynne laughed. "He is so full of himself."

"He knows you're watching," Beau replied. "Everything he does is for attention."

"He's a cutie." She tilted her face toward the sun. "It's so good to be back here."

"You feel up to walking?"

"Sure, I can walk as much as I want, but I can't ride. Doctor's orders."

They fell in step, boots scuffing along the dirt lane that traced the fence line. The morning air was brisk, edged with the smell of hay and burned-off fog. Beau kept an eye on her, not knowing how far along she was in the healing process. It was the first time she'd come out to the ranch since her surgery, and though her steps were slower, she moved with quiet confidence.

"How was your week?" she asked.

"It was great." He stuck his hands in his back pockets. "I finally got smart and handed off part of my work to a couple of the managers. You remember Selina?"

"The young one with the braid? I do. She seemed very capable."

"She is," Beau said. "I let her take a crack at some things I'd been meaning to get to, and she took right to them. It felt pretty good, letting go."

"So you're saying I was right, hmmm?" She elbowed him gently in the ribs.

He grabbed her hand and tucked it under his elbow, pinning her to his side. "And also, I decided to talk to Nate about doing more."

She raised an eyebrow. "Really?"

"I might have been too easy on him, taking everything on myself."

"For all the right reasons, though," she said gently. "You're such a nice guy, and you take pride in handling things. But sometimes you have to let others step up, like you did with Selina. It's no fun being a control freak."

A few months ago, he might've bristled at being called that. Now, he let it slide. JoLynne was blunt, but she was never unkind. That was one of the things he liked most about her. She said what she meant, and he always knew where he stood.

They turned around and headed back to the corral. Leaning against the fence, Beau reached out to stroke Hashtag's mane. "You're hopeless," he muttered, giving the pony a pat on the neck.

"Actually," said JoLynne, "I was thinking he could be useful."

Beau looked up. "Useful? This little hay-burner? How?"

She kicked a rock with her comfortable old boots. "I'm thinking that my friends and I could host an all-day health fair at the park. We could do wellness checks, but also bring in services and vendors from town to talk about what they have to offer. But we need a draw, and Hashtag could be just the ticket. The old people could come up and pet him. Who doesn't love a pony?"

He laughed. "That's what you dreamed up?"

"Literally," she said. "But I think it could work."

"He does get under your skin," Beau said. "Knows how to make people notice him. Might help distract folks from their own worries."

"Exactly," she said.

"But are you sure you're ready for something that big?"

"I think so. I'm healing up fast. And with my insurance background, I've still got a few names to call."

"You think people'll show up?"

"If we do a good enough job publicizing it, yes."

"You'd need shade, tables, parking..." Beau was already thinking through logistics. He couldn't help it—it was how his brain worked.

"There's a lot to think about, but first, I wanted to ask you about Hashtag." JoLynne reached through the bars to untangle a weed caught in the pony's forelock. "What do you think?"

"He'd love it, being the center of attention like that. And he'll go anywhere you are. He likes you."

"Pffft. He likes attention."

"Still," Beau said. "He knows a good thing when he sees it."

"Me, too." JoLynne looked over at him, her gaze soft beneath the brim of her Stetson.

They sat together on a hay bale in the barn's shade, the midday sun heating the pepper trees nearby. Hashtag gave up on them and wandered off. JoLynne laced her fingers through Beau's.

"You're staying, right?" He brushed a hand along her nape and then upward, massaging her scalp.

She groaned at the sensation, and it was all the answer he needed.

As the sun set, they had dinner on the patio, rows of string lights winking in the breeze. The evening was soft with music and the aroma of grilled salmon, and for once, he felt like he didn't need to rush. With JoLynne recovering and things improving at the warehouse, Beau realized he could relax a little.

They ate slowly, sipping their wine and discussing her idea for the fair. They laughed about Vacation Barbie's latest scheme, something about a Mediterranean cruise. And they carefully avoided talk of Nate or the warehouse.

Later, when the stars came out, they climbed into a new hammock designed for couples. Goofy and awkward, they finally got in together and were able to snuggle under the stars.

"I hope I wasn't too pushy earlier," she said. "When I said you should expect more of Nate."

"You were mostly right."

She smirked.

"Don't gloat," he said, laughing. "You've got this way of getting in my head, squawking at me to do what's right."

"'Squawking'!" She whacked his arm, and he laughed and pulled her close.

An owl hooted nearby, and they fell silent.

Because of you, he thought, *I can see myself slowing down. Wanting things I never thought of before. Like time, and peace. And to spend my days figuring out what I can do to make you smile.*

He ran his fingers along her jaw, tilted her chin, and kissed her. JoLynne let out a quiet sigh, and he deepened the kiss, the rest of the world slipping away.

They lay in the hammock for a long time, her head resting on his shoulder, watching for satellites and listening to the night birds sing. The music faded into the background, replaced by the rustle of wind through the trees and the faint sound of frogs starting up in the nearby creek.

He closed his eyes and held her tighter.

The next morning, Beau slipped out of bed before dawn, quietly to let JoLynne sleep. He pulled the blankets up over her shoulder and reached for his jeans. Carrying his shoes, he closed the door, went into the kitchen, and started the coffee maker. A few minutes later, carrying a travel mug, he slipped out the back door, breathing in the cool, damp air. A cow mooed in the darkness, and an owl and its mate hooted back and forth. Beau took a sip of coffee, slid the cap shut, stepped off the porch, and headed for the barn, the gravel crunching underfoot. The sky was still a deep gray-blue, and the quiet was typical of the minutes before first light. One horse whinnied and then came the sound of a hoof smacking a stall door. Beau shook his head.

He slid the door to the side and flicked on the low overheads. Buck gave a soft nicker, and Shorty snorted and tossed her head. Hashtag, naturally, was already craning his neck over the stall gate, waiting impatiently.

"I see you." Beau grabbed a scoop hanging on the wall over the grain barrel.

Hashtag nudged his shoulder in response, more interested in affection than food. Beau rubbed the pony's forehead and leaned into the moment, letting the familiar rhythm of morning chores settle his thoughts.

JoLynne was right. He was carrying too much, but he was determined to change that.

Wouldn't be easy. Beau took pride in being capable. More than that—the guy everybody counted on. But there was something about the way she said it yesterday that stuck with him, saying it was all about control. She hadn't meant it to hurt, but it did sting enough to motivate him.

By the time he finished mucking stalls and tossing hay, the sun had finally crested the ridge. He stepped outside into golden light and stood in the yard for a moment, breathing in the morning. He couldn't imagine not having this. The ranch was everything to him.

But if he wanted to keep her in his life, he'd have to make some changes.

When he came out of the barn, JoLynne stood near the truck, her overnight bag slung over one shoulder.

"What are you doing?" he asked.

"I need to get home," she said. "I've got a busy week, and I want to start planning this Care Fair. But you'll help me think it through, right?"

"Yeah," he said. "Of course."

She looked at him for a long second. "You okay?"

"Sure. Just—" He glanced over at Nate's and shrugged. "A lot on my mind."

JoLynne rested a hand on his chest. "Don't let it all pile up again, Beau. You're allowed to ask for help, you know?"

He gave a half-smile, but his stomach tightened.

"See you soon," she said, and climbed into the cab.

As the dust settled in the driveway behind her, Beau stood for a minute longer than he meant to. The quiet that followed didn't feel peaceful. The ranch felt like a ghost town.

That's when he realized he hadn't seen Nate in nearly a week.

Climbing the steps, Beau felt anxious. He should have checked on Nate. Sometimes, his brother needed a little help keeping to the straight and narrow.

He knocked, but the house was silent.

He waited, then knocked again, harder. Something inside toppled over. Then came heavy footsteps, the click of locks, and the creak of the door as it swung open.

Nate stood there in a tee shirt and sweatpants, his beard scruffy, eyes red. "What?" he asked flatly.

"Wanted to see how you're doing," Beau said, brushing past him into the house.

The place stank. Old takeout, beer cans, laundry everywhere. The smell even clung to the furniture.

"The hell is this?" Beau stood in the middle of the room, hands outstretched.

"Ran outta meds," Nate muttered. "Haven't been sleeping a lot."

Beau started picking up trash and tossing it into a bag. "How come you ran out? Can't you get more?"

"This is my life, brother. If you don't like it, don't come in."

Beau sat down at the edge of the couch and looked at him. "It's not about what I like. It's about what's healthy. This isn't."

Nate didn't answer. He stared at the floor. For a second, Beau thought he might break down. He scooted closer, reached out to squeeze Nate's shoulder. That's when he saw the smirk.

Beau jerked his hand back. "What the hell is funny?"

"You are," Nate said. "You like having someone to rescue, and I'm right here. I always have been."

"You think I enjoy seeing you fall apart?"

"You sure don't walk away," Nate said.

"No, and I won't," Beau said. "What happened to that counseling you were getting? How come you stopped?"

"They were assholes, so I quit."

"You need to do something. It can't be on me all the time. Between you and the ranch, it's a black hole. I'm not going to let it take me down with it."

"Too late, brother," Nate said.

Beau stood up. For a moment, he studied his brother, torn between love and a desire to run away. Then he turned to the door. "I gotta go," he said.

"You mean for good or just right now?"

Beau stared up at the ceiling. As much as he was tempted...but no. He wasn't going anywhere. "Just right now," he answered.

"Then wait."

Nate got up, walked to a corkboard near the kitchen, and pulled off a paper. "I know I'm an asshole sometimes, but do you think you can get this filled?"

Beau looked at the paper, then at his brother. Then he grabbed the prescription and stepped off the porch into the night, the weight of it all heavy in his chest.

Nineteen

JoLynne slipped through the open pool gate, following the hum of voices. Someone had left a pink foam noodle floating in the shallow end. She adjusted the strap of her satchel—book of the month, handouts for the health fair—and braced herself as she rounded the corner.

The door to the library was propped open with a brick, and inside, she could see several of her friends already discussing the book. In the corner, Chuck was setting out three wine bottles and a sleeve of tiny paper cups.

She took a breath.

You've faced worse than a room full of opinionated retirees armed with merlot and folding chairs.

Still, her stomach gave a little twist. Was she really doing this?

For a brief second, she just stood in the doorway, one hand still resting on the metal bar, marveling at the fact that she wasn't winded, sore, or leaning on anything. She had her strength back. Not all of it, maybe, but enough.

Enough to push forward with the latest addition to her list.

Bring healthcare options to the park.

She stepped through the door.

"Come in, come in!" Cass said. "How are you feeling? You look great!"

She and JoLynne shared a quick hug. JoLynne had to smile. Cass was all light and motion tonight, glowing cheeks and laughter, her hair pulled up in a messy bun.

"Gus must be home tonight."

"He is," said Cass. "Go on and sit down. The wine tasting begins in ten minutes."

JoLynne stood next to Cass, taking a moment to study the room. Ursula was sitting near the wine table, back perfectly straight, hands folded over a copy of the evening's book selection. Her gaze swept the room like a security camera. JoLynne gave a little wave. Ursula offered a tight smile in return.

When two unfamiliar women poked their heads through the doorway, looking unsure, Cass waved them through.

"We joined online," said one of them, a woman in a denim jacket with kind eyes. "Can we do this now?"

"You bet," Cass said, beaming. "Make yourself comfortable."

JoLynne watched the exchange with quiet satisfaction. Cass had taken to Serena Cove Mobile Home Park like she'd been born here. Maybe it was the pace of things, or the way people made space for each other, or most likely it was Gus, her new husband.

A swirl of expensive perfume and the crisp click of heels announced Diane's entrance. She wore a flowing black shawl and dark sunglasses, despite the sun having long since dipped below the horizon. Behind her came Teresa and Dan, holding hands, sticking together like Velcro.

Diane took one look at them. Then she lifted a brow. "Men, again?"

"That's me." Dan held open a cooler. "And you're going to be glad because I brought a selection of cheeses from a fancy shop in La Jolla."

Diane raised her sunglasses and peered into the cooler. "You can stay."

JoLynne stifled a grin. Diane's tone was teasing tonight. That was always a good sign.

Kellie bustled in last, balancing a tote bag full of donated books against her hip. "Sorry, I'm late!" she said brightly. "I stopped by the dog park and got ambushed by a schnoodle and two chihuahuas."

"You survived," Cass said, already reaching to help with the bag. "You're a hero."

JoLynne picked a chair near the center and sank into it slowly. She stretched her legs out and crossed them at the ankles, studying her fellow residents, many of whom were changing as the park came together. Diane looked less brittle. Cass looked more confident. Teresa and Dan, still wrapped up in each other, had a kind of settled peace between them now. Even Ursula, stoic as ever, seemed more receptive to being approached.

JoLynne folded her hands in her lap. She would wait until everyone got settled, hopefully with a cup of wine in hand, before she made her pitch.

Cass stood up. "Okay, book clubbers. Let's get started. Tonight, we're talking about *The Alice Network*. But before we dive in, JoLynne asked for a few minutes."

JoLynne sat forward. She'd discussed her idea with Cass ahead of time, and her young friend had been completely supportive, but this was different. This was stepping forward into this group of residents and asking for consensus and their participation. All for the benefit of the less able in the community.

Lacing her fingers on her knee, she took a breath, staring at the floor. Then she looked around the room. "Something's been on my mind," she said. "Teresa brought it up, but it didn't really gel until the other day, when I was helping an elder named Leonard—do you know him?"

Most of those in attendance shook their heads, but Bernie raised his hands. "He's that old guy, lives on the street behind me," he said. "Military man. Sharp's a tack but can't get around much anymore. I asked JoLynne here if she'd help him out, and she's been driving him hither and yon ever since."

"That's right," said JoLynne. "He tried to get in at the VA, but they were too busy. So, I've been taking him over to Teresa's clinic."

"In town," said Teresa. "The low-income place. But we're busy, too, and it's hard for elders to get transportation, so I bring my equipment out here, and I set up in this room twice a month."

"That's really nice of you," said one of the visitors.

"Except nobody comes," said Teresa. "I could do blood pressure screening, all kinds of simple tests, give advice, and provide reassurance if anybody would come."

"What's the problem?" asked Diane. "Do you need publicity?"

"We could use more of that, sure," JoLynne said. "But there are so many services in town that folks here could benefit from, if they even knew they existed."

"I don't get it," said Diane. "Don't most people get their services from their providers? I don't know why we need to do anything. Health care? Really?"

"Possibly. If they can afford it and if they have transportation and IF they are capable of managing their own situations," said Teresa.

"Which brings us to my idea." JoLynne looked around the circle. "What would you think about hosting a health fair?"

There was a beat of silence. Diane removed her sunglasses, folded them, and slipped them into her purse. "Here?"

"In the park," JoLynne said. "Probably in the ballroom. Saturday morning, maybe four to six weeks out. It wouldn't be huge, but we'd pull together what we can. Wellness screenings, information tables, and health services vendors from in town. Teresa knows people at the clinic. We could make it easy and useful."

"That is ambitious," said Ursula.

"It is," JoLynne admitted. "But I think we can do it. In fact, I mocked up some flyers imagining what the fair could encompass, if you want to take a look." Reaching into her satchel, she withdrew a stack of papers and handed them to the women beside her to distribute.

Cass read her copy and then held it up in the air. "This looks fabulous. I vote yes. It could be amazing. Think of how much good we could do. We might catch someone about to have a heart attack!"

Diane glared at her.

"We could get a nutritionist," said Teresa. "Maybe someone who works with older adults."

Dan raised his hand halfway. "I could offer to do fire safety inspections if they're worried."

"You're hired," said Teresa. "Promise you'll wear your uniform."

He beamed at her.

Diane gave a low snort. She stood up. "Assuming this is more than just talk," she said, "who's paying for tables, permits, and insurance if someone trips over a yoga mat?"

"We are," JoLynne said. "As treasurer, I can confirm that there's money in the budget for such community support activities. Because the previous board never allocated it."

"I'm so glad I persuaded you to take that position," Diane said, rolling her eyes.

JoLynne laughed.

Teresa leaned forward. "You know," she said gently. "It's a fine idea, and we'd all be there, but what if it's just us and a bunch of tables full of brochures?"

"It's all about the publicity," said Cass. "We've got a decent mailing list now, and I can help with flyers and a landing page on the park site."

"I can reach out to my clients," Kellie added. "They're always willing to spread the news of community events."

"We need a draw," said Bernie. "Dunk tank? Raffle tickets?"

"Actually, I have a secret weapon." JoLynne reached into her purse and pulled out her phone. She tapped a video file and turned the screen toward the group, handing the phone around. As the guests viewed the screen, JoLynne heard a chorus of "aww" and "how cute!"

Because on the screen, Hashtag the pony trotted into frame, tiny hooves kicking up dirt. He wore a red halter and a straw hat with cutouts for his ears. His cinnamon coat gleamed, and he strutted as if he knew he was being filmed. Beau's voice was faint in the background, coaxing him.

Hashtag paused, then shook off the straw hat and proceeded to eat it.

"Oh my god," Kellie said, "that little guy is adorable."

"He's a showman," JoLynne said. "And people love animals. If we bring him to the fair, folks will come out just to pet him and take pictures."

"You can bring him?" Diane asked, still recovering from a laugh.

"Beau said he'd help, as long as it's outside and he's got a place to tie Hashtag when things get hectic."

"Seriously, though," Cass said, looking around the room. "This is gold. We could post a teaser on the community site."

JoLynne stuck her phone in her purse. "We've got time to plan it right. Long as you're all in."

A quiet murmur of agreement moved through the group. Even Ursula gave a small nod. Diane exhaled.

"All right," she said. "He's got more stage presence than both of my ex-husbands. I'm in."

Chuck raised a bottle of wine. "Is this a good time?"

Cheers erupted, and a line formed at the round table. Diane slipped out of her seat and joined Chuck at the table, helping to hand out samples as he described what they were tasting.

JoLynne caught Teresa's eye. The meeting had begun with a book, but it was ending with something else. Energy, laughter, and a shared sense of purpose.

Cass had gently redirected the group back toward the book discussion, wrapping up with next month's book, volunteer reminders, and a suggestion from Kellie about pet adoption day.

In time, chairs scraped back from tables. Sweaters were pulled on, good-byes were said. Bernie and his helper, Leland, said goodnight and went out the door.

Chuck headed for the door with his sack of empty wine bottles. Diane followed him, her finger hooked in his belt, shawl gathered dramatically around her like a cloak. "Well, I can't say I expected a pony as an incentive for the old people, but here we are."

"Good night, Diane," JoLynne said.

Dan and Teresa followed, their hands linked, speaking softly. Kellie was already out the door, calling goodnight over her shoulder.

JoLynne turned back toward Ursula, who stood at the far end of the room, still seated in her chair.

"You need a ride?" she asked, keeping her voice light.

Ursula stood slowly, pushing her chair back into place. "No, thank you. I brought my cart."

Her tone was perfectly polite, but there was a finality in it.

JoLynne nodded. "All right. Are you up for more swimming lessons? My doctor says I can, if I go easy."

"Yes." Ursula stepped past her, shoulders straight, chin high.

Cass was waiting by the pool gate as JoLynne flicked out the lights. "Do you need a ride?"

Cass shook her head. "Gus will be here any minute."

"Okay, if you want to wait."

Cass slung her purse over her shoulder. "This was a good idea, Jo. Thanks for caring enough to suggest it."

"I think it could be," JoLynne said.

"No. It already is. Oh, hi, honey!" Cass jumped in the cart next to her husband and waved goodbye.

JoLynne switched off the lights and locked the door, then the pool gate. When she finally stepped out into the parking lot, the night was soft and mild. The streetlights buzzed faintly. She walked slowly toward her cart, sandals tapping on the blacktop.

Before she opened the door, she glanced back.

Ursula stood alone beneath the walkway light, arms crossed, face tipped toward the sky as if she were listening for something beyond reach. She didn't move when JoLynne looked at her. The image stayed with JoLynne long after she turned the starter key.

The click of the lock echoed in the silence as Ursula stepped into her home and locked the door behind her. Everything was in its place, exactly as she had left it. The narrow glass vase on the entry table still held a single stem of eucalyptus, dried now, perfectly intact. She slipped out of her shoes and walked barefoot over the tile. She hung her sweater on the hook near the door, flicked on a lamp, and crossed into the kitchen.

The house was cool and quiet. The thermostat glowed a precise seventy.

Ursula bypassed the kettle and went to the sideboard, where a single bottle of aged whisky stood beside one carefully chosen glass. She poured a measured amount and set the bottle back in place with a soft clink.

Crossing the room, she pressed play on the stereo. A cello suite rose up, precise and low, filling the space like a hymn. She sat in the leather wing chair beside the bookshelves, angled slightly toward the window. Her glass rested in one hand, the other folded in her lap as she sat listening.

Book club had gone well. JoLynne had handled herself capably. The pony video had been absurd but effective. Even Diane had laughed. Cass, as always, had sparkled. Ursula, meanwhile, had said very little, simply observing as was her way.

She finished her drink and placed the glass on the low table beside her chair. Standing, she studied the bookshelf. Her fingers slid along the spines until they found the one she hadn't touched in months: a slim, cloth-bound German poetry collection, faded at the edges. It opened to the right page.

The passport was crisp and rigid, renewed just before she moved into Serena Cove. Somehow, she couldn't imagine being without one.

Amir's email had contained an itinerary, forwarded from another address. His message, as expected, was short and inoffensive.

The apartment is spacious. It has a view. Stay as long as you like.

Istanbul. He would be there for six weeks, and after that? He didn't know. They never knew.

Ursula stood motionless in the center of her living room, passport in hand. The silence pressed in gently, like the fog creeping in over the land from the ocean.

She turned off the lamp, and the room went dark.

Twenty

Unloading the dishwasher the next morning, JoLynne wondered how one person could make so much work for herself. She bent down carefully to put a kettle in its cabinet. Still, it felt good to be on her own, alone in her cozy house, breathing in the salt air as the morning warmed. She could hear the distant crash of surf through her open kitchen window, and if that didn't make a person happy, there was no hope for her.

Reaching up to put away a stack of dishes, she paused for a moment to study her list, which she'd moved from the refrigerator door where anybody could see it. Now, it was hidden in the kitchen cupboard.

JoLynne broke out in a wide grin. The sense of accomplishment was gratifying. Her list was coming along.

Some items had been added right after Gene died, and after careful consideration—join a club, go dancing (she'd done that on the ship), get involved with the park. One, try online dating, didn't seem important anymore now that she was seeing Beau. With a sigh of relief, she crossed that one out.

The others, impulsively scribbled onto the end—ride horses again, learn to swim, have sex—were also progressing in their own uneven way. The last one was the reason she'd moved the list. No sense in scaring the neighbors.

The one that made her happiest was the one about sex. But it was more than sex. JoLynne had a boyfriend, even if his life was pretty chaotic. She worried about Beau, that he was trying to do too much. But he'd have to figure that out on his own. If she'd learned anything in her old age, it was that you couldn't force people to grow and change.

She closed the cabinet door and looked around her kitchen. It wouldn't make it into *Architectural Digest*, but with the sun-warmed linoleum, the chipped sunflower bowl on the counter full of keys and paperclips, and the blue ceramic mug still steaming beside the sink, it was hers.

In her younger years, she might have aspired to a grander house, fancier cars, and better clothes, but now she simply valued health, peace, and friendship more than anything.

And that she could support herself, even if she'd never be rich. Her finances had stabilized with her government pension, the errand-running business, and part-time work in the park office.

Coming out of the semi-isolation that so depressed her while caring for Gene, it was enough to smile and wave at other residents, walk on the beach, hang out at the clubhouse, and drive her golf cart home to her cozy double-wide with pale yellow siding and new curtains in the front window.

It was like a little oasis.

Still, there was Gene's room. One of these days, she would get to it. The medical supplies had been taken away, but there were still boxes and suitcases full of what he'd arrived with. Gene never married the other woman. He had no children. No surviving relatives. Which had made JoLynne feel even sorrier for him.

Now that crap was her burden to offload.

Clean up Gene's stuff.

She scrawled it at the bottom of the list, then closed the cabinet door. While spending time with Beau, she'd been able to shove Gene's situation to the furthest reaches of her mind. Beau was good at distracting her with horses and ranch life, but it wasn't a solution.

Her phone buzzed on the counter.

Swamped. Talk later?

She stared at it for a moment.

Then she shook her head and went to get ready for her day. She was excited to get started on the Care Fair. Today she would go into town and meet with businesses that might be interested in having a table at the event. But first, she'd promised to check in on Leonard.

She finished dressing and grabbed her keys. The last time she spoke with him, he seemed interested in helping with the fair. She was not sure how much he could do in his situation, but if it kept his spirits up, she'd find something.

The sun had already burned off the morning marine layer as JoLynne eased into Leonard's driveway. She grabbed her canvas bag and climbed the shallow steps, hearing the faint sound of the television on to a news channel inside. The front door was open a crack and the smell of coffee drifted out. She knocked gently on the screen.

"Door's open," he called out.

Inside, Vera, his daughter, was standing at the kitchen island, making a salad.

Leonard sat at the table, hunched slightly in his chair, sorting pills into a day-of-the-week container with trembling hands. His white cardigan was spotless, and his hair was neatly combed.

He looked up and smiled. "How are you this morning, my dear?"

"Great! I wanted to stop by and compare calendars, to make sure I know what you've got coming up this week."

Leonard nodded, reaching for a spiral notebook. "Let's see. We have the podiatrist next Monday, groceries Tuesday, and the barber on Thursday."

JoLynne pulled out her own planner and sat down across from him. "That matches what I have, but also, didn't you say something about an optometry appointment?"

Vera stopped chopping cucumbers. "I'd help, but I've got to find a new job."

JoLynne looked up. "What do you do?"

"Whatever I can find," said Vera, placing the salad container in the fridge. "My last job was home health aide, but I got grabbed on the ass one too many times, so I've been bunking at Dad's until I can find something new."

"Vera's a hard worker, if you hear of anything," said Leonard, scribbling something with a pen bearing the Marine Corps logo.

"I might," said JoLynne. "Will you be living here in town?"

"Who can afford that? This place is ridiculous. Only rich people welcome." Vera marched down the hall, shutting the bedroom door hard.

"Sorry," said Leonard. "She can't seem to get ahead."

"Can she live here for a while?" JoLynne asked, her voice barely above a whisper.

"Not too long." The old man gave a mock shiver. "She's opinionated. Needs her own place."

"Tough situation," she said.

"I can hear you, you know," Vera said loudly from down the hall.

"She's had more lives than a barn cat." Leonard sighed. "I wish we could figure something out."

Vera returned to the room. "I'm sorry I slammed the door. I'm just stressed out. If you hear of anything..."

"I'll put some feelers out for you," said JoLynne. "Now, I should go. I have some people to see in town."

"Thank you for stopping by, and I'll see you next Tuesday," said Leonard. "Unless Vera can take me."

"Hopefully, I'll be in the wind by then, Pops." She planted a kiss on his head.

Climbing back into her SUV, JoLynne headed for town, wondering how Beau's day was going. The text wasn't a good sign, but she had faith in him. In their own ways, they were both trying to find a new path. And then, hopefully, they could move forward together.

The catwalk outside Beau's office vibrated faintly underfoot as a couple of workers hurried past in their steel-toed boots. Beau tapped his radio and brought it to his mouth. "Sam, did you sign off on the Davison shipment yet?"

Sam, his trainee, said, "Uh, I thought Darnell was lead on that."

"I'm looking at the assignment board and you're it. We need that broken out and processed today, okay?"

"You got it, boss."

Beau let go of the button and stepped outside his door. Down below, two forklifts passed within inches of each other. They should know better. He made a mental note to talk with Jason about his guys.

He exhaled wearily. This was supposed to be the part where he let go and reaped the benefits of letting other people handle things.

Wasn't a hundred percent working out that way.

Some of his changes were promising. Selina was a born leader, but she was in Burbank all week for management training. Ava Martinez, also solid, was back from maternity leave but still only working half-days. On top of everything, the summer beach flu was making its rounds.

His phone rang. One of his customers hadn't received a shipment of building materials needed to start work. With apologies and promises, he hung up and stared at the phone like it might contain the answer.

This was the cost of stepping back, wasn't it? For a moment, he missed the old days when he did everything himself, stayed late, and made sure everything ran right. It was hard, and the work was nonstop, but at least he knew what was going on.

There was a knock on the glass. Walters stood at the door with a clipboard.

"We have a labeling issue on the C-range pallets," she said. "Want me to rerun them or wait for QA?"

He paused.

Walters didn't look unsure. She was offering him a choice of whether he'd like to step in or let her handle it.

"Go ahead and rerun," Beau said. "I'll message Lisa."

He turned back to his computer and opened the messaging app. For all the craziness, Beau had to admit he liked it when his people came to him to check, to solve problems, to ask for advice. It was exciting to be in the middle of the action, and he felt better knowing where all the landmines were buried.

Not that JoLynne would agree.

As he typed out a message to his QA manager, his phone buzzed with a text. He eyed it, hopeful it was her.

But it was Nate. Something about today's feed delivery.

Beau finished the work message and called his brother.

"The guy's here right now," said Nate, "and I don't really understand the problem."

"They screwed up our order a couple weeks back, and it keeps reoccurring," said Beau. "Want me to talk to him?"

"I'll put him on," Nate said, his voice worn down.

It was an easy fix, something Nate should've handled if he wasn't having a bad day, but sometimes, the past rose up and grabbed him by the throat. When that happened, he wasn't much good to anybody, and his only recourse was to rest.

Beau didn't blame him, but that didn't make it easier. After hanging up, he sat back and stared at the ceiling, feeling like a loser. If he let go of too much, the wheels came off. If he held on too tight, well, that was no life either, he was coming to realize.

He didn't know where the sweet spot was.

He thought about JoLynne, how she always made things sound simpler than they were. Questioning his long hours, nudging him toward balance.

The problem was she didn't know what it took to keep all this running.

He needed to figure it out for himself, and he would, just as soon as he got a little time to think.

Any day now.

Twenty-One

J oLynne hadn't felt this accomplished in a long time.

The week had been a blur of phone calls, printed flyers, Google Maps, vendor lists, and tiny victories that kept her riding high. The health fair was turning into a real event, not just an idea on a community bulletin board.

On Monday, she'd spoken to a woman at a regional chiropractic clinic who had already blocked off the date. Tuesday brought a tentative yes from a mobile blood screening outfit. They just needed to confirm the electrical access on-site. On Wednesday, she cornered the guy who ran the smoothie stand by the pier and got a firm maybe. As of Friday morning, she had eight confirmed vendors and two who said they were very likely.

And then Cass texted her the flyer mockup, and it made her laugh out loud in the park office. Right at the top: a photo of Hashtag the pony, looking noble and vaguely confused beside the words "Healthy Living in Serena Cove!" in cheerful blue. Cass had posted it on the park's new social media feed, and within an hour had six likes, two shares, and one offer to adopt the pony.

Cass responded with, "Sorry, Hashtag's owner wouldn't want you to do that," and it made JoLynne laugh.

Teresa had compiled a list of services to prioritize, including blood pressure checks, dental referrals, fall-risk screenings, and Medicare info. Ursula was doing what Ursula did best: turning chaos into order. She'd deputized Chuck and Dan to track down folding tables and chairs and even gotten them to repaint the chipped A-frame signs they used for event parking.

It felt like everyone was pulling in the same direction. JoLynne took a moment to savor the feeling. It was nice being part of something again. She'd missed that. Tonight, she was going to celebrate by doing something simple and entirely selfish: going to dinner with her boyfriend.

She still felt odd calling him that. At their age, it sounded like a punchline or a typo, but there wasn't a better word for it. Beau wasn't a fling. They saw each other every chance they got, texted often, and talked about deep subjects. Sometimes they'd read the same book and talk about it afterward. He was an intelligent, complex, caring person, and her heart lifted when she saw his name on her screen.

Now, standing in her bedroom mirror, JoLynne leaned close to apply lipstick and give herself a critical once-over. The top she'd chosen was soft and flattering. She'd washed her hair and blown it out the way she used to before she got dragged down by caregiving.

Tonight, the effort wasn't entirely for Beau. She stared at her reflection, and the woman in the mirror cracked a little smile.

It felt good to take care of JoLynne again.

She stepped back from the mirror and turned toward the hallway to grab her purse just as her phone rang. Seeing Beau's name pop up gave her a moment's thrill, but that warmth disappeared the second she registered his tone of voice.

"Hey," he said, his voice tight. "I'm so sorry to do this, but I need to raincheck dinner."

Her first instinct was irritation, but then he clarified.

"There was a fire," he said. "At the ranch. I got off early to get everything ready for our date, but when I was a few blocks away, I saw the smoke."

"What happened? Are you guys okay? What about the horses?"

"Yeah, it happened in the tractor shed. We got it stopped, but the tractor's a complete loss."

"I'm so sorry. Is everyone alright?"

"Nobody got hurt, but Nate's pretty upset."

"But he's okay?"

"Physically," he said, exhaling sharply. "Mentally, he's in bad shape. He was supposed to do a cleanout last week. There was a pile of oily rags or something flammable wedged behind one of the workbenches. It ignited somehow, probably from a worn-out extension cord."

She perched on the couch arm, rubbing her temple with her free hand. "How extensive was the damage?"

"Luckily, the neighbor spotted the smoke early and called it in before it spread. By the time the fire department got there, Nate had a hose on it."

"Jesus, Beau."

"I know."

For a moment, neither of them spoke. JoLynne could hear the background hum of voices behind him, the occasional metallic thud of tools or doors closing. She got a mental image of the ranch, with smoke curling into the late afternoon sky, flames licking wood, and horses terrified. Her stomach twisted.

He spoke again, softer now. "I'm sorry. I really wanted to see you tonight."

"Stop," she said. "Don't apologize for putting out a fire."

"Still."

"Beau. Look, I'm glad everyone's okay. That's all that matters. We can have dinner anytime. Just go and do what you have to."

"Maybe next week?" he asked, and she could hear the exhaustion in the question. Like someone barely above water, too tired to plan but too polite to leave it open-ended.

"We'll talk about it," she said. "I can meet you for lunch one day. I know you can't predict your evenings."

"That'd be great," he said. "Yeah. That'd be good."

"Are you okay?" she asked again, more gently this time.

There was a pause. Then, with something like quiet self-loathing, he said, "I should've double-checked the shed. I told Nate to do it, and he half-assed it. I knew it. I should've just done it myself."

"Beau, you can't watch every aspect of two lives at once. Especially when one of those lives is hurting." She hated hearing guilt and self-recrimination in his voice. "You've got a ranch, a brother who needs you, and a whole team counting on you at work. You can't be in ten places at once."

"Yeah," he said. But it didn't sound like agreement.

"I mean it," she said. "Be kind to yourself, okay?"

"Trying," he murmured. "I'll call you."

"Okay."

And then the line went quiet.

She stood in her living room in her nice blouse, with her purse dangling from her shoulder and her lipstick a little too bright now. She set her purse down on the entry table and stood there for a minute, just listening. The house was quiet, and her reflection in the darkened front window looked like someone waiting to be let in. She toed off her flats and walked barefoot into the kitchen, conscious of the pretty outfit she'd chosen with such deliberate care.

"All combed and curried with nowhere to go," she said to herself.

The wine she opened was already chilled. It was one of the good bottles she'd been saving for a nice dinner. She poured a modest glass and took it to the couch, lowering herself onto the cushions with a sigh.

JoLynne took a sip and stared across the room at nothing in particular. She wasn't angry. Beau hadn't blown her off. He'd had a real emergency and had no choice but to deal with it.

She was sensitive to the fact that he had so much on his plate, but she'd encouraged him, maybe even leaned on him a little, trying to get him to have Nate take on more. So Beau could make room for a life beyond work, a life that included her.

Had she pushed him too far? Was she being selfish, not really taking his obligations seriously?

She took another sip, letting the quiet stretch out, letting her mind work.

He was doing his best. She believed that. But it was beginning to look like his best didn't leave much room for her. What scared her most was the creeping sense that maybe it never would.

Was that okay with her? She was older and semi-retired. She had her own place, her own life. It wasn't like she needed a man to start a family with, or to tell her how to think or who she was.

JoLynne wasn't twenty anymore. Those days were behind her.

She'd spent so much of her adult life looking out for men who needed her but didn't care about her. Gene, with his sorry stories and sickbed apologies, was only the latest. He hadn't cared about her as a person.

And yet, she'd taken care of him in his last days. Why? What did she get out of it?

Well, she did have a feeling of satisfaction that she had done the right thing, even if he didn't deserve it. Living here in Serena Cove showed her what happened to people who didn't have anybody in their most vulnerable moments, and JoLynne would never hate herself for what she'd done.

At the very end, Gene, with his bristly old chin quivering, his eyes red with brimming tears, had reached for her hand and told her thanks and that he was sorry. That's what she got.

That, and a pile of his old belongings in the guest room that she'd been avoiding.

She didn't want to be needed like that. Not ever again.

But she also didn't want to walk away from someone who was going through a rough stretch and who was beginning to matter very much to her. Lately, when she thought about her future, he was there, too. He was worth the wait.

She looked down at her glass, half-empty. The lipstick print on the rim felt like a little joke.

On impulse, she reached for her phone and tapped Vivian's name.

It rang twice before that familiar voice answered: "Friday night and you're calling me. This can't be good."

JoLynne laughed softly. "Yeah, well. The night kind of unraveled."

"Did he cancel?"

"There was a fire at the ranch."

Vivian let out a low whistle. "How bad?"

"Just the equipment shed, but they lost a tractor."

"Hope they have insurance."

"Nobody got hurt, which is a blessing. Just that everybody's pretty upset."

"Well, yeah." There was the sound of Vivian taking a sip of her beverage. "How are you doing, Sis?"

JoLynne paused, and then she spilled her guts. When she finished, Vivian asked, "So you're sitting there all dressed up having a sad little glass of wine?"

"Basically."

"I hope it's a good glass of wine."

"It is. I was saving it for tonight."

"Of course you were." Vivian exhaled into the phone.

JoLynne swirled the wine in her glass and stared at the little crescent left behind on the rim. "I'm not mad," she said. "I mean, how could I be? It was a fire. An accident. But I'm sad. And I feel stupid for being sad. Which makes me more sad."

"Welcome to love at our age," Vivian said. "Less drama. More internal complexity."

JoLynne stopped, frowned, and started again. "I had lectured him about taking some pressure off himself and giving Nate more responsibility. So then, this happens. He's beating himself up—"

"And I guess you are, too," said Vivian.

"Pretty much." JoLynne took a deep breath. "I don't want to walk away just because things are hard. But I also don't want to keep making allowances forever. Been there, done that. I think I'm too old to take that on again. To shout encouragement from the sidelines while I wait for somebody to make better choices."

"So tell him that."

"I can't. He had a fire, Vivian. He doesn't need me piling on."

Vivian was quiet for a beat. Then: "You're a mess, aren't you?"

"I guess I am."

"You really care about this guy."

JoLynne closed her eyes. "I guess I do."

"Listen," said Vivian, "why don't I come down for a couple days? We can walk the beach and drink wine and stare at the ocean until things make sense again."

"You can do that at your house."

"Yeah, but you're not at my house."

JoLynne smiled, grateful. "Okay. Yeah. Come."

After they hung up, she changed into her sweats and streamed a movie. When it ended, she set the wineglass in the dishwasher and wandered through the house, checking doors and turning off lights.

Wandering barefoot, she stopped at the sliding glass door, watching the dark shapes of eucalyptus trees sway against the city-lit cover of clouds.

Somewhere beyond her yard, she could hear the hush of the waves pulling back, gathering themselves for another surge.

She didn't know what she'd say to Beau. She wasn't sure if she should back off or stay strong for herself. She only knew that tonight, a point of change had been reached.

And tomorrow, she'd have to decide what to do about it.

Twenty-Two

J oLynne knelt on the carpet and braced one hand against the wall as she wrestled a stubborn box free from the back corner of the closet. It resisted, wedged between an old suitcase and a toolbox covered with a faded towel. She gave it a sharp tug. It came free all at once, dumping her on her butt. "Dammit," she muttered, sitting up. "That wasn't helpful."

One corner of the box was crushed, the writing on it smudged but still legible.

TAHOE CRAP.

She blew a strand of hair off her face. Lake Tahoe was where Gene first went when he left JoLynne for the warehouse secretary. She didn't want to open it. Nothing good would be found in that box. Or this entire room, for that matter.

Gene's room. Where the air always smelled like plastic tubing and microwaved soup. Now, just the faint stink of a room that had been closed too long. The bed was gone. The machines, the pill bottles, the quiet beeping. Only his boxes remained. A battered laundry basket slumped against the wall. A small dresser listed forward on uneven legs.

Since Gene had no children and no surviving family, it was entirely up
to her to decide what to donate or trash. She figured she'd earned that right
after three years of housing and caring for him.

Now she stood, nudging the box with her toe. "I don't know if I have
the stomach to go through this one, Viv. If you wouldn't mind."

While her sister attacked the box, JoLynne continued removing clothing
and containers from the upper shelves. It was dank, unpleasant work.

Vivian pulled open the box flaps. "You worried for nothing. It's just a
bunch of old shoes and a bowling ball. Which I guess were important in
Tahoe."

"That's just sad," said JoLynne.

"More like pathetic," said Vivian. "For a man who was basically home-
less, he sure left behind a lot of junk."

"I'm going to get more water," said JoLynne. "Do you want some?"

"Yeah, bring me a bottle, too," said Vivian, shoving the box aside. "Are
you keeping this nightstand?"

"Soon as it's empty, it goes out on the curb," said JoLynne. "I'll be right
back." In the kitchen, she grabbed a couple of bottles out of the fridge. A
chicken casserole was thawing, good for tonight's meal. She was grateful to
have her sister there. Even though she had no attachment to Gene anymore,
getting his stuff out of her house was like putting to bed the last several
decades of her life. Wondering if, to some degree, she had wasted it. In
that sense, it was painful, but there was no sense lingering in the pain. She
carried the water bottles back down the hall.

Vivian was standing in the middle of the room. She was holding a phone,
still attached to a charger. "I found this behind the nightstand," she said.
"It was plugged in."

"That must be Gene's," said JoLynne.

"He probably plugged it in here and forgot about it." Vivian pressed
the button on the side. The display lit up, Gene's face angled badly at the
camera. "Geez, dude, trim the nose hairs," she snorted.

JoLynne held out her hand. "Let me see."

"You going to go through it?"

"I'm curious." JoLynne sat on a box and swiped up. There was no passcode. She tapped the screen. Vivian peered over her shoulder as various apps opened. Photos, to start with, many of them of Gene and people she didn't know. A boat on Lake Tahoe. A classic car. A woman clutching her hat and laughing, sitting on his lap.

JoLynne's chin dropped to her chest.

"Is there any reason to keep going?" asked Vivian.

"I guess not." JoLynne handed the phone to her sister. She needed to keep moving forward, not dwell on the past. "Do we just throw it in the trash, or what?"

There was no response. JoLynne turned around. Vivian was staring at the phone, her mouth forming a silent O.

"What?" JoLynne reached for the phone. Together, they stared at the screen. It was a text thread.

Gene:

She's got a good house, warm bed. Somebody's going to get her. Might as well be you.

Beau:

Don't talk about this.

JoLynne blinked. She opened her mouth to say something, but no sound came out. The air around her seemed to thin, as if they were at altitude and she couldn't catch her breath. Frozen, she stared at the screen until it went black.

Vivian gently took it from her hand, powered it down, and dropped it in the trash. "We need to get out of here."

JoLynne looked up, her mind blank. "What?"

"Let's go for a walk." Taking JoLynne's hand, she pulled her out of the room and shut the door. Wordlessly, they padded down the hall to the front door and slipped on their sandals.

JoLynne followed Vivian down the dirt path from the clubhouse to the beach. Slipping out of their shoes, they carried them to the water's edge, turning north to walk along the wet, cold sand. The surf rushed in and hissed back, sometimes rising over their ankles, other times disappearing.

They didn't speak. A gull cried overhead and JoLynne looked upward, following its path along the shoreline. She adjusted the sleeves of her light sweater, pulling them down to her wrists. The wind off the ocean made her eyes water.

Half a dozen surfers bobbed in the distance, light shapes in dark water. The sky was clear blue, mocking JoLynne with its cheerfulness.

"You know what the worst part is?" Vivian said finally.

"I'm sure you're going to tell me." JoLynne didn't look at her.

"The worst part is that I'm not surprised. That text was Gene, through and through. He only wanted you for your paycheck."

"You trying to make me feel better?"

Vivian kicked at a mound of sand. "I feel like I have some authority here, being on husband number four."

A faint lift at the corner of JoLynne's mouth. It barely qualified as a smile.

Vivian went on. "So let me tell you about Mr. Four. He's got more money than God and a heart like a calculator. No feeling."

"I thought this one was going to stick," said JoLynne. "What happened?"

"I haven't loved him in years," Vivian said, softer now. "When I realized that, I rationalized that I was staying for the security. I like traveling, and I think he likes it when I'm gone. Makes it easier on both of us."

"That's very sad." JoLynne stopped walking. A gust of wind blew her hair into her face, and she scraped it back.

"I'll be okay," said Vivian. "And you know what? I could use a travel buddy."

"Aren't we a pair." JoLynne reached for Vivian, and the two sisters shared a long, teary-eyed hug. They broke apart and began walking again. The waves rolled in, white foam curling around their ankles.

"Thing is," Vivian began, staring straight ahead, "you're free now, Jo. If you want to be."

JoLynne's throat moved, but no sound came out. She gave the faintest nod.

Later that evening, JoLynne stood at the open patio door for a moment, watching her sister out on the deck. Vivian was curled into one of the cushioned chairs, bare feet tucked under her, wineglass balanced on the armrest. Her hair lifted in the breeze. She looked peaceful. JoLynne wished she felt the same. Behind her, the house hummed softly and the grandfather clock chimed the end of day.

JoLynne went back inside, opened the bedroom door, and took the phone out of the wastebasket. She flopped on the sofa, staring at Gene's text.

Sure, Vivian was right. Gene was always a shit, and JoLynne was a fool to fall for him. But that was over.

Except now it wasn't.

Beau's reply was so lackluster as to be complicit. Why hadn't he pushed back? How come he didn't tell Gene exactly what to do with his invitation? Even though Beau hadn't known JoLynne very well, wouldn't you slap down the person who made such a horrible statement?

But Beau hadn't pushed back. Hadn't stood up for her at all. Hadn't demonstrated even the most basic human decency.

On the other hand, the Beau she knew was kind, self-sacrificing, even. It was hard to reconcile the two. Add in her lack of faith in her own judgment, it came out to a big, fat no.

She stared at the text thread for a moment, then took a screenshot and sent it to Beau's number. A long breath left her, slow and quiet. Would he respond or just cringe and avoid her from this point on, forever? She waited. The clock over the sink ticked. Sighing, she started to get up when her phone rang. She jumped slightly before answering.

"JoLynne?" His voice was low, intimate. "I saw the message. It's horrible, but that was Gene's idea, not mine."

She said nothing, trying to assess how she felt.

"Are you there?"

JoLynne exhaled an annoyed puff of air. "I'm here."

"I didn't want that conversation," he said. "I tried to shut him down, but I didn't fight with him over it. Gene said a lot of things, all the time. We got used to it. Nobody took him seriously."

"Your secretary did."

"I am sorry. She was, well, the two of them were a match. Guess I don't need to say more."

JoLynne cut right to the chase. "Is this why you came to see me? To move into an empty parking space?"

"Come on," he groaned. "You know better than that."

"I really don't," she half-laughed. "Not really. Not anymore."

"This is crazy that you would judge me like that. Haven't I shown you who I am?"

JoLynne's voice softened. "Yeah, you have."

"I'm am sorry," he said. "I always hated the way he treated you. He was such an arrogant jerk."

Against all odds, JoLynne smiled. "He was."

"And maybe in some way I thought I could make it up to you. When I brought you the photo, I was just being nice. I didn't realize anything would come of it."

"Me neither." She stared out the window, past the patio lights, to the edge of the darkness beyond. Vivian must be getting cold. She was probably staying outside to give JoLynne space.

He hesitated. "Babe? Talk to me."

"Listen, Beau, you've been through the mill. You told me how your ex left you and the kids, and how it hurt them. The man who stuck around and raised them, that's the Beau I know, not the man who'd wimp out when some bastard says bad things about a perfectly nice wife."

Beau didn't answer.

"But it has shaken me up in ways you can't even imagine," she said.

"I understand."

"No, you don't." Anger tightened her jaw. "I was married before Gene."

He was silent for a moment. "I didn't know that."

"Because I don't talk about it," she said. "That guy found a good house and a warm bed, too. You'd think I'd learn."

"Jesus," Beau said, under his breath.

She gave a tired little exhale. "I'm a little like you. I like to help. Sometimes, it's too much, but I can't see it. I'm trying to see it now. To take better care of myself."

Beau tried again. "Look, JoLynne, I'm not sure how to fix this. But I have never lied to you or tried to manipulate you. All along, I've just been trying to do the right thing. Be a friend. That's it."

"I don't know what to think," she said.

"Just please don't shut me out." There was a knock on his end. A voice in the background.

"Are you at work?" she asked, incredulous. It was the weekend, after seven in the evening.

"Yeah," he muttered. "That's my foreman. We're wrapping up some last-minute stuff. Can I call you later?"

"It's already later."

"Tomorrow, then."

"I don't care." JoLynne hung up and sat silently in the darkening living room. Then she slid open the glass door to join her sister.

Vivian looked up from her wineglass. "Well?"

JoLynne sank into the chair next to her and pulled the blanket off the backrest, draping it across her lap. Her fingers worked the edge of the fabric while the wind combed gently through her hair. A gust stirred the wind chimes dangling from the patio cover. They jingled softly.

"I don't know if he's on the up and up," JoLynne said. "Or just trying to come out clean."

Vivian nodded. "Might be both."

"He said he hadn't wanted any part of Gene's plans. That he always felt sorry for me."

"He what?" Vivian growled.

"The way Gene treated me. He saw it for years."

"So he's been dating you out of pity?"

The waves crashed below the bluff, louder now, thumping down onto the sand.

JoLynne leaned back in her chair, letting her eyes close.

"I'm sorry, Sis." Vivian reached over, warm fingers curling around JoLynne's hand.

Twenty-Three

A dozen agendas, stapled and smoothed at the corners, sat on the kitchen table. JoLynne straightened the stack for the third time. She didn't need to make physical copies since most people barely skimmed them, but today she needed something tangible. Something she could hold and point to. Something that would keep her from thinking of Beau.

Vivian had left that morning after a heartfelt breakfast together, in which the two of them made a pact to stand up for themselves in the face of uncaring or untrustworthy men. JoLynne had dressed with determination. She would move forward, throw herself into the park, and minimize, if not forget, the tall, handsome rancher who was probably just looking for a payday.

No, that was too harsh. But maybe not? She couldn't trust herself to decide.

The ballroom at the clubhouse was quiet and cold, still musty from the dampness. She flicked the light switch, brightening the mood a little, and began arranging chairs on both sides of a folding table.

At the sound of footsteps, JoLynne turned to see Teresa hurried in, sunglasses stuck on her head, a bottle of water clutched in one hand.

"You're early," said JoLynne. "Thanks for being here."

"I wanted to get as much done as possible," said Teresa, glancing at her watch. "We have career day at the clinic later."

"Did you ever ask Vera if she wanted a job?"

Teresa frowned. "I couldn't pin her down. So I guess not."

Cass and Gus arrived next. He carried a shallow crate draped in a checkered cloth. "I told her we maybe could bring a bunch of these to the fair," he said, lifting the cloth to reveal a dozen heirloom tomatoes, streaked gold and red, each one still dusted with a bit of soil. "First pick of the season. Totally organic."

Cass smiled up at him. "You can take the boy out of North Dakota..."

JoLynne reached for one of the tomatoes, weighing it in her palm. "These are beautiful. People will love them."

Gus looked quietly pleased. "Might be others in the park who'd want to contribute. I can bring a folding table."

"A farm stand!" said Kellie, coming through the door. "This is getting better and better."

Chuck came in carrying a cardboard coffee tray. "We bought extra if anybody's missing out on their morning caffeine."

"I'll take one," said Bernie, arriving with Leland at his elbow.

A smiling Diane slid around behind Chuck, brushing comfortably against his shoulder, and began distributing the coffee.

JoLynne blinked. Diane, smiling?

Ursula appeared without a sound and took a seat, chin up. She caught JoLynne's eye and gave a brief nod.

Soon the room was buzzing as participants and volunteers arrived and took their places. JoLynne raised a hand in the air and called out, "Can we get started?"

The buzz quieted. She stood instead of sitting, wanting to make eye contact with everyone in the room. "Thank you for coming," she began. "We are four weeks out from the fair, so today is to discuss vendor logistics, confirm volunteers, and assign backup coverage where needed. I'd like to keep this meeting under an hour."

Teresa nodded without looking up from her phone. Gus tapped Cass's list, pointing to a name.

"Okay, then." JoLynne moved to the first bullet on the agenda. "Dan, were you able to confirm the fire department's food truck will be there?"

"Got it right here," he said, holding up his phone.

"Great. Chuck, are you still good for parking lot control?"

Chuck opened his mouth, but before he could answer, Diane spoke. "Actually, we won't be here for the fair," she said lightly. "Chuck and I are taking a trip."

JoLynne frowned. "You're not going to be here?"

"We're driving out to Four Corners." Diane beamed at Chuck. "In his RV!"

"That's right." Chuck sipped casually from his coffee cup.

"Together?" It was out before JoLynne could stop herself.

"Sure," Diane said, with a shrug that tried very hard to be nonchalant.

There was a beat of silence.

"Oh," JoLynne said. "Well. That means we'll need someone else to handle tent layout, sanitation, and the mobile mammogram bus."

Diane reached across the table and drew a line through her name and Chuck's.

"Let's move on." JoLynne moved briskly to the next item, trying to outrun the part of her brain that was still stuck on Chuck and Diane. "Next subject is volunteer stations. We need to decide who's covering what during the early shift. I've got Roni on check-in and Jordan helping with setup."

Roni, Teresa's daughter, chewed on the end of a plastic straw. "We're planning on doing that at least until twelve-thirty. Then, Jordan has to bounce."

One after another, the volunteers began bowing out—Roni had to leave early, Jordan had drills, Ursula might be overseas, and Dan's granddaughter was due any minute. Even Kellie's niece was backing out of face painting.

JoLynne pressed her fingers to her temples. "Anyone else have surprise travel plans, impending births, or firehouse exercises I should be aware of?" She looked around the table at their smiling, unconcerned faces and felt something in her chest go taut. The event was unraveling, but no one seemed to care.

And she was about to make everything worse.

JoLynne flipped the page and paused, tapping her pen once before making her announcement. "Animals and children's activities. I'm sorry to have to say that the pony won't be able to attend."

"What?" Cass asked.

"I meant to text you, Cass, but it's been a hectic morning."

"No Hashtag?" Roni made a sad face. Jordan reached for her hand.

"We were so looking forward to him," said Kellie.

"He's been acting up lately," JoLynne said, ready with a plausible excuse. "Nothing serious, but a couple of little scares. He tried to buck during grooming last week. I'm not sure he's a safe bet for crowds."

Cass frowned. "Shoot. I already told people he'd be there."

"Well," JoLynne said, standing a little straighter, "everything else is still on track, though, right?"

Diane raised an eyebrow, but said nothing. Ursula looked out the window.

JoLynne wanted to fold up her materials and go home.

Teresa stood. "What is the deal, everybody? You were all so gung-ho when we first talked about it, but now you're bailing. Please tell me you're going to make an effort, because this is important. This could really help the park!"

JoLynne looked at Teresa and quietly said, "Thank you." She gazed around at the group. "When I moved in here, it was a graveyard. A ghost town. Nobody talked to each other. Bunch of for sale signs rusting on people's front lawns. I wished it was nicer back then, but I had my forty-hour-a-week job and didn't have all that much time to worry about it. Then my ex moved in with me to die, I lost my job, and it was even less important. Because at the time, you know, I was just surviving."

She looked around the room at people who had become friends. Several nodded sympathetically.

"But now I'm okay," she said. "Things are getting back to normal." She swallowed, the lie choking off her voice for a second. "Anyway, this fair is important for so many of the folks in the park. If we want it to be a good, happy place to live, we really should follow through with our plan. If you're still going to support it. But if not, tell me now and I'll start canceling the vendors."

She looked down at her agenda.

Chuck frowned and then turned to Diane. "Maybe we could delay our trip a few weeks?"

"Fine, I guess," she said, gazing into his eyes.

"I can ask my coworker to switch things around a little," said Roni. "If that would help."

"Thank you," said JoLynne. "It would."

"The food truck's definite, so no worries there," said Dan. "We'll have barbecue in the parking lot as promised."

"I might be able to bring puppies," said Kellie. "If a certain client of mine will let me, we can do an adoption thing to take the place of the pony."

The planning wrapped up, and people started leaving.

JoLynne felt her shoulders come down from around her ears. She allowed herself to let go of the resentment that had been building and let gratitude take its place. This was what she had hoped for when she first moved in: community. Earlier this morning, it felt like everything was falling apart, but maybe not.

Vivian's voice came back to her. "You could always just go on another cruise."

The thought hovered, as unreal and distant as a postcard. Blue water. Sun. No agendas. No one dropping out or smiling like everything was fine while the wheels came off.

Somehow, it had all ended well. The Care Fair was on.

JoLynne gathered her papers. This morning's drama had been just what she needed, a good distraction from heartbreak.

Sometimes you had to take what you could get.

Twenty-Four

The leather bridle was dry and cracked along the browband, curling like a leaf that had outlived its tree. Beau sat in the shadow of the barn's west wall, elbows on his knees, turning the old bridle over in his hands. Dust coated the stitching. One of the cheek straps had split where the buckle met the loop, a thin tongue of leather peeled back from the core.

It was early evening, Monday. The heat was starting to loosen its grip, but the barn still radiated warmth like a stove cooling down. The horses were quiet in their paddocks, tails flicking. The fragrance of eucalyptus and pepper trees wafted around the paddock on a breeze.

He could fix the bridle. He had the tools and the know-how. It wouldn't take much. But his hands didn't move. He just sat there, turning it over, again and again, as if the answer to everything might be hiding in the split grain of old leather.

JoLynne hadn't texted or called, and he was trying to give her the time she needed to figure things out. Or maybe he needed it himself. Beau still couldn't believe she'd assumed he was the same kind of dog as Gene. But that was her right. If she wanted to let him down, sell him short...wasn't his call.

The sun was throwing longer shadows now. Tonight would be the third Zoom meeting. The first two had been discouraging. A group of people who sounded too wrung out, too exhausted to help themselves. One middle-aged lady cried for the whole hour. One of the younger guys apologized every time he spoke. Beau had sat through them because he said he would.

He checked his watch. 6:57. Shit. He stood up slowly, knees popping, and hung the bridle back on its hook to wait another month or two for him to decide what to do with it. He dusted off his jeans, stomped his boots on the porch, and headed inside. "Third time's the charm," he muttered.

He would keep attending because if he stopped, Nate stopped.

The fight was two weeks ago in the kitchen at Nate's house. It was a bad one, almost the worst. The kind where furniture nearly got involved. It started with fence work and ended up with Nate saying Beau needed to find money for the sprinkler system.

Beau had shouted, "I'm sick of carrying this whole goddamn place on my back!"

"You think I don't know that?" Nate had shot back, his face red. "You think I like having you haul me around like a pack mule?"

"Then do something about it," Beau shouted. "Stop being a victim!"

"You should know." Nate's voice dropped.

The two brothers stared at each other.

That was the moment Beau lost his momentum, sunk by the weight of it all. The futility and hopelessness of trying to save everybody and everything single-handedly. He pulled out a kitchen chair and fell into it, leaning back, one hand rubbing his forehead and then scrubbing through his hair in frustration. Then he shook himself and looked up at Nate, who was staring into the living room, silent now.

For a second, profound sympathy washed over Beau. He cleared his throat.

"I'm sorry about everything that happened to you, brother, but I can't fix you."

"You sure try, though."

"I do. You're right."

"Well, stop. Just leave me the hell alone."

One of the horses whinnied, the sound crossing the yard through the open window. Beau loved that sound. He wondered how long he would have it.

"You always think you're the good guy," Nate said quietly. "Like you're the hero in some sad cowboy movie. You think that makes you better than me?"

"Maybe I should go," Beau said. "Maybe I should stop worrying about it. Sell the horses and let you have it."

"Maybe you should."

Beau shoved the chair back and walked out without another word.

In the morning, Nate was on his porch with a tray of blueberry muffins. "You got a few minutes?" he asked when a surprised Beau opened the door.

"I have to leave for work," said Beau.

"Thought about it all night." Nate shouldered past him and set the tray in the kitchen. "I'll try therapy. But only if you do the same."

Beau had scoffed. "What the hell do I need therapy for?"

"Figure it out," Nate had said. "Figure out why you can't stop fixing everything. Why you think you're the only thing standing between us and disaster."

So Beau had signed up for a low-cost online codependency group that met Monday nights on Zoom. There were about eight of them there, all with sad stories. Beau kept his mic muted the whole time.

Now, he set his beer down and logged on, the screen blinking to life. Five faces already there. Someone was talking about her daughter's meltdown at a Father's Day picnic. Another about being the emotional trash can for his coworkers. Beau slouched deeper into the couch.

He'd already decided to bail after ten minutes when she came on. The speaker was a woman in her late fifties, hair stringy, no makeup.

In a soft voice, she related her sad situation at home, to which Beau barely listened. But then she wrapped it up by saying, "If everyone around me is okay, then I feel safe. I've always been that way and I wish I could stop."

Beau froze, looking at the screen. Her voice was so flat and defeated that it landed like a brick to the chest.

She kept going. "I learned early that if people were calm, I wouldn't get hurt. So I got real good at keeping people calm. I kept peace between my parents, my husband, my boss, my kids. I got so good at it, nobody noticed I was exhausted. I didn't even notice. I just knew that if things were peaceful, I could breathe."

"Shit." Beau sat up, wiping his mouth with the back of his hand.

She was telling the story of his life.

The warehouse, the ranch, his kids, Nate, JoLynne—every situation, every person, every relationship. He hadn't been trying to help so much as trying to level everybody out so he could feel safe.

It was all about him.

He sat perfectly still, feeling the horror and hope of self-recognition. When the hour ended, he closed the laptop, stood slowly, and walked into the kitchen. He poured two fingers of bourbon, took it out to the porch, and sank into the old swing.

The midsummer sky had gone to dusky lavender. The wind had finally picked up. A rooster crowed in the distance. He sipped his bourbon, feeling the burn going down his throat, replaying what he'd heard, what it meant. That woman was talking about him.

He wasn't a hero. He was scared.

Beau stayed outside long after his glass was empty.

The next night, he brought pizza over to Nate's place. He hadn't asked if Nate needed pizza. He just knocked on the screen door and walked in with the box.

After preliminary small talk, they ate in silence. Eventually, Beau wiped his hands on a paper towel and said, "I'm thinking of moving."

Nate raised an eyebrow but didn't interrupt.

"I'd like to find something closer to work, someplace small that I can rent. I'm tired of driving."

"How would you still work here, though? Seems like that would just make it harder."

"That's the other thing. I think we should find help. They can rent my house cheap for doing what I do on the ranch."

Nate closed the pizza box, folded it, and jammed it in the recycling. "I don't like it. I already told you that."

"Yeah, I know, and I'm sorry, but I need to make a change." Beau stared down at the table. "I'd include you in the interview process. Make sure you're okay with whoever we pick, because it's not just a renter, it's a ranch hand."

Nate walked over to his back door and stood there, hands in pockets, gazing out at his weedy yard. Then he heaved a big sigh and said, "I'm going to say yes, not because I'm that cool with it, but because I think it'd be good for you."

Beau blinked. That was more than he expected.

Nate came back to the kitchen. "The guy I'm seeing, the therapist, he's smart. He's a veteran, too. I kinda wanted to hate the bastard, but he's got some decent ideas."

"Like letting me leave?"

"Like letting you leave."

Beau stood up and cleared the table, his throat tight.

Then Nate said, "You planning to move in with your girlfriend?"

Beau shook his head and tried to smile, but couldn't quite get there. "She's long gone."

"That's too bad," said Nate. "She was okay."

"Yeah, well." Beau turned toward the door. "I'll try to get some interviews set up for next weekend, if that's okay with you."

"That works. Wait a second."

Scraping his chair back, Nate stood and approached him, his hand extended.

Beau shook it, and then stepped into the cooling night, letting the door close quietly behind him.

Twenty-Five

The midsummer breeze blew from the warm inland valleys, and JoLynne was sweating through her blouse.

"Dolly, you absolute brat," she muttered as the miniature horse side-stepped the halter for the third time. "You do this every morning. What's the deal?"

Dolly gave her a look, an eye roll in equine terms, before relenting and letting JoLynne slip the halter over her scruffy ears. She was the size of a large Labrador with the attention span of a five-year-old at a birthday party.

JoLynne felt lucky to have found Blue Mountain Rescue. Always needing volunteers, the owner had her get started right away. The smell of dust, hay, and horses was putting something back together in her soul.

"You just have to look pretty for ten minutes," she told Dolly, stroking the white blaze on her nose.

"She'll behave once the cameras are out," said a voice behind her.

JoLynne turned to see Wade Dunn, one of the sanctuary's co-founders, leaning on the fence post with a currycomb in one hand and a half-eaten apple in the other. At eighty, Wade looked like someone had hung barbed wire and canvas over a steel frame and called it a man. His skin was weathered, and he'd probably been lifting hay bales since the Kennedy administration.

"Looks like her publicity team is here," JoLynne said, angling her chin toward the two young women who occasionally posted on social media about the sanctuary. It was good for drumming up support, so the founders let them.

Wade bit into his apple and chewed, eyes squinting against the morning sun. The sanctuary sprawled behind him. It was located inland a few miles from the ocean, and comprised rolling paddocks, weathered fencing, and a white barn with peeling trim. She liked it here. Two weeks in, she'd stopped checking her phone every ten minutes because the mini horses kept her too busy. There were about thirty of the little guys on the property, but Dolly was the star.

Tending to the horse, JoLynne and Wade worked in sync, like old teammates. Wade handed her a clean lead rope without asking. JoLynne passed him the hoof pick mid-motion. His pace was unhurried, and he had an easy way of talking that made you feel like whatever you were doing was right.

"You going to stick with us for a while? We could use the help."

JoLynne shrugged. "As long as you don't fire me."

"You show up on time and don't let the horses escape. That's ninety percent of the job right there." He gave her a sideways look. "And it looks like you don't mind getting dirty."

"I've got three kinds of hay in my bra right now."

Wade laughed and looked away.

They brushed Dolly in silence for a few minutes, the horse twitching and snorting dramatically with each pass of the brush. When Wade moved around to clean the hooves, JoLynne caught sight of the sanctuary's small office building at the top of the slope. A flicker of motion behind the curtain meant Wade's wife was in there, probably sorting bills or calling around for donations.

"How's Fran this morning?" JoLynne asked.

"Mad at the printer. Believes it's personal." He gave Dolly's hoof a thump and lowered it gently.

JoLynne liked Wade and Fran. There was no fuss to either of them. They had run the sanctuary for twenty years, saved every animal they could, lost plenty of money and time, but kept going anyway. They had no time for self-pity and no tolerance for showboating. It was a good environment for someone like her, just beginning to remember who she was at this point in her life.

They finished with Dolly and led her back into the paddock. The horse trotted off indignantly, then dropped to the dirt and rolled as if she hadn't just been brushed.

"She's going to be filthy in twenty seconds."

"That's the dream." Wade leaned on the gate, watching her loop a lead rope with practiced ease. "You know your way around a barn."

JoLynne hooked a foot on the low rung of the corral fence. "I grew up on a ranch in Montana. My dad kept horses for working the cattle, nothing fancy. Although I did compete a little in high school."

Wade tipped his hat back. "You don't forget that kind of thing."

She glanced over. "No. I can't live without the smell of a barn. Sweet hay, leather, the animals. Coming here brings it back."

Wade nodded. "Fran and I had a place outside Salina, Kansas, when we first got married."

"How long ago was that?"

"Fifty-nine years and counting." Wade straightened, brushing off his jeans.

"Wow." JoLynne looked at him. "That's quite an accomplishment."

"All credit to Fran," he said, "puttin' up with me."

JoLynne hung up the rope, hiding her face. She felt the ache in her chest and caught her breath. It was still there. Of course it was.

She picked up the bucket of brushes and headed into the barn, determined to shake it off.

A couple of hours later, she was home, showered, and changed into comfortable clothes. In the kitchen, she opened her laptop to work on the health fair. Soon flyers, printouts, and notes from Teresa and Cass were scattered across the table.

After her initial panic, it looked like all the ducks were once again flying in formation. The fair was a week away and looking good. A surprising number of local businesses had reached out—some even wanted to refer their own clients. After a quick consultation with her team, JoLynne was happy to open it up to all comers.

She just hoped Kellie would be able to bring the puppies, since Hashtag wasn't coming. She felt bad about getting everybody all excited about the pony, so it would help if they found some cute little pups to replace him.

Her fingers hovered over the keyboard. For a few seconds, she didn't type. She looked at her phone instead. Nothing. No missed calls, no texts. No stupid little cowboy emojis.

Clearly, he was giving her space. So much space that she was about to float off into the universe, untethered.

JoLynne looked across the living room and out through the slider. The patio was bathed in late afternoon light. Even after wearing herself out at the minihorse sanctuary all morning, she still felt restless energy buzzing through her.

She got up and paced to the slider and back. What the hell was wrong with her? She gave herself a few more seconds to glare at the phone, to pretend the signal was bad, or that he'd lost his charger, or was trapped under a tractor somewhere.

But no. This was Beau taking her at her word. He was treating her the way she'd asked to be treated.

Damn him anyway. Gentle, respectful Beau, waiting for her to make the first move.

It pissed her off. If he truly felt wronged, that she had blamed him unfairly for Gene's text, shouldn't he put up some kind of fight?

But men like Beau didn't argue or plead. They disappeared. They ghosted with dignity.

Good riddance.

Sure, tell yourself that, she groaned. *You don't miss him at all.*

For a moment, she let herself remember the way he said her name when he was half-asleep. How his hand knew the shape of her hip in the dark. The way they made love, with a kind of aching slowness that made her feel precious.

She shook her head. Dangerous thoughts. JoLynne had wanted to feel like a part of something again, to feel as if she mattered to someone. But that need was a fragrance that could waft around a woman like pheromones, attracting the wrong person. That was how Beau found her, after all. With that damn picture Gene left at the warehouse.

Maybe that was Beau's lucky day when he discovered that photo. He'd found a way in.

Her stomach twisted. She didn't want to believe that about him—or about herself.

She crossed the kitchen, tugged the elastic from her hair, and stood in front of the mirror in the hall. Although she saw shadows and lines, deepening now into what Vivian laughingly called crevasses, JoLynne was still pretty. Attractive in a way that took time to develop, and Beau had responded.

But she'd been a fool before, choosing men who saw her competence as their convenience. As if she were an appliance. A labor-saving device to make their lives easier.

Well, she'd learned her lesson. Gene had been a master class.

That last night at the ranch with Beau, when he talked about how hard the commute was getting, she'd almost asked him to move in. Just blurted it out, right there under the influence of the sunset and the stars. Then she'd stopped herself because she was learning to be cautious. To wait until the other person proved themselves first. It helped her feel safe, like she'd finally learned something.

But maybe JoLynne had learned the wrong thing. Maybe she'd learned to protect herself to an unhealthy degree. Maybe her walls were too high. So what if he was looking for love and rescue? Why was it bad for her to be the hero? She was capable, and she liked the feeling. As long as she kept some kind of balance between service and sacrifice.

Keeping Beau in her life was a risk, but so was letting him go.

Twenty-Six

The late morning sun was already relentless by the time Beau stepped out of the barn, coffee in hand, and stared at the front gate like it might magically produce a responsible adult looking for work. No such luck.

The final interview had just ended twenty minutes ago, and he still felt like he needed a shower.

The guy—Ray? Roy?—had smelled like corn chips and beer, and seemed deeply offended by the idea of paying any rent at all, given he was expected to also do ranch chores. It was a very small amount, but Nate had suggested they at least charge something to validate a legal relationship.

"Otherwise, they're squatters," Nate had said, a leftover instinct from his almost-lawyer days.

Beau had smiled politely at Ray/Roy, showed him to the gate, and then locked it behind him.

Shorty was nosing around by the trough, and Buck was dozing in the sun. Hashtag stood at the fence waiting for attention. Beau reached out to pat the shaggy pony on its neck.

Hashtag leaned in. His mane was doing its usual porcupine impression, and Beau was tempted to laugh, but it was too much effort. He rubbed a hand over his face, then down the back of his neck. He was tired. Not bone-tired, not like after the divorce, trying to raise a couple of kids and hold down a job. But tired in a way that told him he was ready for things to change.

And he was working on it.

"I just need to find somebody to take my place here," he said to Hashtag. "If I could get out from under all that, that'd be a game-changer."

"You talking to yourself again?"

Beau turned. His brother was barefoot, coffee in hand, squinting like he hadn't been up long, though his voice sounded clearer than it had in weeks.

He descended the porch steps slowly, his gait steadier than usual. "You get any more candidates?"

"Nothing any better than what we saw already," said Beau. One guy looked like he'd be cooking meth out of the tack room by Tuesday. Another had four hound dogs in his truck and wanted to know if Beau would be okay with them roaming.

"That family in the van was a sad case," said Nate.

"Yeah." One applicant had arrived with his wife and three children. He was surly and rumpled, and although the woman's hair was combed, her clothes looked like she'd slept in them. It appeared that the family was living in their vehicle. All five of them.

"She looked real tired," Beau said. "She was smart, though. Smarter than him, for sure."

"Rough life," said Nate.

"Yeah." Beau rubbed his chin. "I feel bad, but... it's not gonna work. Not here."

Nate nodded, accepting that. "It's not our job to save everybody."

Hashtag whinnied.

Beau looked over at him again. It was Saturday, the day of the Serena Cove Health Fair. He wondered if JoLynne was already there, clipboard in hand, running around making sure everything went smoothly. He wished he could be there helping her, but it was critical to attend to ranch business.

And to leave her the hell alone, as she'd requested.

He hadn't heard from her since the breakup. Not a text or a phone call. She wanted space, and he was giving it to her. God help him.

Beau sat down on the top step of Nate's porch. His brother sat in a chair nearby. The whole ranch felt still, like it was waiting for him to do something, anything. He thought about cleaning out the back shed again. Thought about going into town for supplies.

But he just stood there, watching the dust dance in the light, Hashtag's shaggy body pressed against the rails. He was starting to wonder if this whole "giving her space" thing was just a cover for his own fear. For staying put. Because if she thought he didn't care, or wasn't willing to fight for her—

Hell, maybe that was worse than crowding her. Worse than showing up when he hadn't been invited.

He stared at Hashtag, still pressed up against the fence like he had nowhere else to be. Beau knew the feeling. JoLynne had wanted to bring the pony to the fair. Said it might help draw the older residents out, give them a reason to come by and get the care they needed.

That had meant something to her, but now the idea was collateral damage to their relationship drama, drama the old folks didn't deserve.

"You know," he said to Nate, "I've got this crazy idea to go for a ride."

"Shorty could use the exercise," said Nate.

Beau stood up. "Do you know where we stuck that old pop-up canopy?"

Nate thought about it. "The green one? Might be in the back of the workshop. Why?"

Beau moved off, Nate walking along with him. Dragging open the creaky door of the workshop, Beau flicked on the overhead light and inhaled the familiar scents of oil and wood shavings. The canopy was buried under a tarp, next to a stack of faded folding chairs and a milk crate of bungee cords.

Trying not to breathe, he and Nate hauled it into the open air. It was dusty but serviceable.

"Do you want help?" Nate asked.

"Sure." Beau reached into his pocket and tossed him the keys. "You could line my truck up with the horse trailer."

The smell of kettle corn hit JoLynne first. That was a nice addition to the fair, courtesy of Teresa's friend who owned the candy shop in town. "Where's Diane?" she called out to Cass.

"She's printing name tags," Cass answered, both hands full of folding chairs. "Or setting fire to them. I honestly don't know."

It was ten minutes to start time, and the community lawn was a hive of motion: booths going up, volunteers dragging signs into place, Ursula scolding someone about shade positioning. To her absolute shock, JoLynne realized Ursula's friend Amir was the one taking directions, letting her boss him around like he hadn't just negotiated some nuclear disarmament treaty.

Or something.

JoLynne watched them from a distance, Amir speaking gently, leaning down to look at her, eye to eye. Ursula letting go of a tightly held smile, Amir laughing out loud and wrapping her in a hug.

It took JoLynne a beat to realize her friend was smiling. She felt her throat tighten unexpectedly. Ursula, who made no demands, who'd built a fortress of a life, was nestled in Amir's arms.

It made JoLynne's chest ache a little.

She spun on her heel and took her clipboard away to the farthest booth on the edge of the lawn. Most of her team had shown up despite her fears.

With one exception, but that couldn't be helped. Since she'd run him off.

She stood beside the information table, hands on hips, clipboard tucked beneath one arm.

It had been Diane's brilliant idea to forgo the ballroom and just set up all the booths on the lawn near the pool. They'd encouraged the vendors to bring shade protection, and with all the pop-ups circling the lawn, it looked more like a craft fair than a health fair. A blood donation bus idled nearby, welcoming anyone willing to give. The pop-up shade for the puppy adoption booth was protecting an empty pen, unfortunately, because the yellow lab had been late having her puppies and they were too small to bring. The Zumba instructor's Bluetooth speaker was pumping out salsa music, adding a festive air.

Against all odds, the Serena Cove Mobile Home Park First Annual Health Fair was coming together.

People were smiling. Balloons were floating. There was the fire department's food truck, with Dan manning the twin barbecues.

"Hey, this looks like fun," said Vivian, bumping JoLynne with her shoulder.

JoLynne couldn't help but smile. It was more than even she had imagined. Under a deep blue sky and puffy white clouds, the aroma of salt water and barbecue was intoxicating.

When this was all over and she got home, she was going to take her list down and throw it away. Every item had been checked off, and more. JoLynne felt as if she had remade her life.

And then she saw a white pickup easing down the narrow access road, a faded trailer hitched behind.

Twenty-Seven

A white pickup truck came through the front gates, hauling a beat-up silver horse trailer behind it. It rolled slowly toward her, coming down the narrow road leading to where she stood on the clubhouse lawn, the fair's banner flapping overhead. Two men were in the front seat. The driver waved.

Beau.

Her heart caught.

When the truck reached the clubhouse, it swung left. In the passenger seat, his arm hanging out the window, Nate waved.

"Holy moly," JoLynne whispered.

"Is that your friend?" Kellie, beside her, shaded her eyes.

JoLynne didn't answer. She slapped the clipboard into Kellie's hands and started walking toward the rig.

On the far side of the lot, the truck swung around until it faced the exit, the trailer bumping gently behind it. The engine fell silent. The driver's door opened.

Beau stepped out, reached back inside for his Stetson, and turned to face her.

He wasn't smiling. Just holding still, like maybe if he moved, she'd vanish.

Her steps slowed.

From inside the trailer came the stomp and whinny of a very impatient pony.

Beau held out his arms.

And JoLynne went to him.

They stood like that a moment, her face buried in his chest, inhaling the reassuring scent of aftershave and sunlight. "I didn't think you'd come," she said quietly.

"I wasn't sure I'd be welcome."

She leaned back and gazed up at him. "Always."

The ramp thudded onto the blacktop, and Nate ducked inside. He unclipped the lead rope from the fixture and turned Hashtag around, leading him down the ramp. The horse raised his head in the direction of the fair. His nostrils flared, and he whinnied.

"Think he's after the caramel corn," said Nate, tying the pony to the side of the trailer.

JoLynne's laugh bubbled up and spilled over, and Beau gave her a squeeze before going to help Nate.

JoLynne took Hashtag's rope. He nudged her with his long nose, rubbing his forehead against her shirt. "I missed you, too," she said.

"Here, this is yours." Kellie slapped the clipboard back into JoLynne's hands and focused on the pony. They led Hashtag, his hooves clopping on the blacktop, toward the fairgrounds. Chuck was waiting on the curb. "There's a spot under that jacaranda tree, over there," he said. "What do you think?"

"I think it'll work great. Thank you." JoLynne guided Hashtag up over the curb and to the shady place on the lawn.

Almost instantly, visitors were gathering around, wanting to pet him. Beau and Nate returned from the truck with hay bales on a dolly, arranging them in a half circle for seating as the elders came over to enjoy visiting with the charismatic pony. JoLynne handed Beau the lead. He took it from her, their eyes locked, hands touching, neither wanting to move away. Gazing up at Beau, JoLynne felt something settle inside. It felt like hope.

Reluctantly, she slipped away to tend to the fair while Beau and Nate introduced Hashtag. It amused her how a little horse could bring out the kid in anyone.

She made her way past the booths, answering questions and giving directions. Teresa was doing blood pressure checks. Diane was handing out brochures. Dan, manning the food truck grill, waved a pair of tongs in her direction. JoLynne waved back, heart full.

In the swirl of laughter, music, and ocean air, she gave herself a quiet pat on the back. *You did this,* she thought. She tilted her face to the sun, smiling. Life was good.

Returning to her duties, she spotted Ursula and Amir sitting side by side on the bench overlooking the ocean, their heads together in quiet conversation. As much as she would hate to lose Ursula, JoLynne hoped her friend went away with the handsome Middle Easterner. The two of them had so many adventures still in front of them.

As she watched, they rose from the bench and, hand in hand, followed the path that led down to the beach.

"Our spot's available," said a voice behind her. She turned to see Beau coming up behind her. "Want to join me?"

She craned back in the direction Beau had left Hashtag. "How's Nate doing?"

"He and some woman named Vera are holding down the fort."

"Vera?"

"She offered to take my place. Tried to pretend it was about the pony, but I'm not sure I believe her." With a little smile, Beau held out his hand.

JoLynne took it. The breeze picked up her hair and tossed it across her cheek, and she didn't bother to fix it. They arrived at the bench overlooking the crashing surf. He rested his arm behind her, and she snuggled close.

"This is really an amazing view," he said. "You must feel lucky to come out here any time you want."

"I don't take it for granted at all," she said.

"Do you think anybody would notice if a nonresident used it from time to time? Like after work, on his way home to his apartment in Serena Cove?"

"I'll be damned." She leaned back to look at him. "You mean it?"

"Yep." He looked a little embarrassed. "We found somebody to live in my place and help Nate. There'll be a training period until it gets easier, but then it should be good for everybody."

"And you won't have to commute."

He brushed the errant lock of hair out of her eyes. "That's part of it."

They sat quietly for a moment, watching a pair of gulls swoop down toward the water.

"I came to a conclusion too," she said, voice low. "About us. Well, about me."

"Tell me."

"Thing is," she said, "I like to help." Her voice barely audible, she cleared her throat and began again. "I told you I was married twice, and both were bad deals. But I decided to quit beating myself up. From time to time, I might have been helping the wrong person or doing too much, but I'm not going to stop. I need to be more careful, but I enjoy helping."

"Like me." Beau lifted her hand to his mouth and held it there.

"Yes, like you. We are similar that way."

"It's a matter of balance, I guess," he said. "Knowing when to quit."

She turned to him. "I never thought you were the type to take advantage. But I wasn't sure. I'm sorry about that. I know better now. At the time, though, I had to get away to protect myself."

"I knew I was stuck," he said, "but I couldn't figure out what to do about it." He stared out at the ocean, holding her hand against his thigh. "Nate tricked me into finding the answers."

"He's a good brother."

"So now that we're both unstuck," he said, "do you think we could move forward together?"

She looked at him sitting there against the backdrop of the California coastline, a good man who had put too much of a priority on being strong for everyone around him. The man with a heart that was almost too big, who had once shown up with a photo and invited himself into her life.

"I think we could," she said, taking a slow, deep breath. "But there's one last thing still on my list, and I would very much like you to help me with it."

Twenty-Eight

J oLynne hadn't seen a sky like this in years.

The stars weren't lightly scattered like in southern California, struggling to be seen through the marine haze and city light. Here in Montana, it looked as if a giant had thrown handfuls of diamonds onto the endless blue-black velvet nighttime sky. It brought back so many memories.

Beau sat beside her on the porch swing of the dude ranch cabin, one boot heel scuffing the wood. The two of them were as comfortable together as if they'd grown up on neighboring ranches.

In the distance, the lowing of cattle drifted faintly from one of the pastures. The resident dogs had finally gone quiet. Nearby, someone was playing a gentle guitar, the notes so slow they seemed suspended in mid-air.

Beau tipped his head back. "I think I get it now."

"Get what?"

"Why people make such a big deal about this place. It's so beautiful and open. You can really breathe."

She leaned her head against his shoulder. "It's bittersweet, though."

They'd been at the dude ranch three days, and the two of them were having a blast. Earlier that day, they'd ridden side by side through a golden stretch of valley, red-tailed hawks coasting overhead. A few of the other guests had ridden along, as had a guide. When they reached the river, an elegant lunch was waiting for them on white-linen tables for two.

Another day had involved tricks and training at the corral, where Beau had tried roping a dummy calf on wheels, but the thing was radio-controlled and it hilariously continued to evade him. JoLynne laughed so hard she snorted.

The ranch was rustic in all the right ways, with good-natured horses, group meals cooked over open firepits, and individual guest cabins in a wood-and-iron motif. In other ways, it was as indulgent as a five-star hotel, with a clawfoot tub in the room, a bar that had an evening bourbon tasting, and bedsheets softer than a whisper.

JoLynne had been a little skeptical when he'd agreed to her idea. This was Beau Landry, a man who once claimed his idea of self-care was changing the oil on time. But here he was, purposefully on vacation, laughing at the staff's corny jokes and riding horses to the trout stream for a fly-fishing lesson.

Since they'd arrived at the ranch, they'd spent almost every minute together, but it wasn't too much. When she felt the need for a solo walk yesterday, Beau had occupied himself in the resort's library, a quiet place with comfy leather chairs and a wall full of books.

Now, on their last evening, they lounged in Adirondack chairs, staring into the flames of the private fire pit behind their cabin.

"Have you gotten any calls from work?" JoLynne asked.

"Not one," he said. "I told Selina to only call me if the warehouse burned down. And then only because I wouldn't have to come in on Monday."

"You are really getting with the program," JoLynne marveled.

"What about you? Think you'll do another fair next summer?"

"Maybe sooner." The health fair had been a huge success, partly because so many of the residents came out of their homes to socialize instead of remaining isolated. In addition, townsfolk had shown up as well, curious about the fair and the community.

"It was satisfying to tell people about services in town they hadn't known of before, like Teresa's clinic and the senior workshops. And now they know that if they don't have transportation, that's not a problem."

"Because of your new business." Beau held his hand out, palm up, and she laced her fingers through his.

"And Cass is planning to start a computer and technology support service with help from the local high school. There's so much to be happy about."

"There is," Beau sighed. The fire crackled, and somewhere in the distance, two owls hooted back and forth.

They sat for a long time like that, with no pressure to fill the quiet. JoLynne closed her eyes for a moment, breathing in the scent of juniper and wood smoke. The warmth of Beau's hand holding hers. The hush of the mountains surrounding them.

And yet, something was tugging at the edge of all this goodness. Just to remind her there was something left to do, painful though it might be. And she'd promised Vivian.

"Before we leave tomorrow," she said, "I want to visit Joshua's grave."

Beau turned to her, his eyes soft. "Do you want me to come with you?"

"Please."

That night when they turned out the lights and snuggled under the quilt together, their lovemaking was hungry at first, then steady and tender, as if they were finding their way home, one touch at a time.

In the morning, JoLynne felt stronger, ready to face the day.

They packed their bags and checked out, leaving well before they were due at the airport. The rental car was quiet except for the radio, which drifted in and out with old country songs that felt familiar.

The cemetery was on the edge of town, just off a rural road flanked by weathered white fences and lush green grass. It was small, simple, and surrounded by cottonwood trees. It felt forgotten, and JoLynne's eyes stung.

She held a small bouquet of wildflowers in one hand, Beau's hand in the other. Silently, they walked to the gravesites, a path she knew from memory, even though it had been years. Stopping in front of the three headstones, she crouched down by Joshua's grave, her palm on the warm cement, her eyes closed. There was that moment, like falling. A tiny collapse inside her chest.

She thought of the last time she'd seen him in all his eight-year-old sweetness. His clear skin was pink with excitement as he saddled his pony, ready for a ride with his big sisters, so happy to be included.

The little guy hadn't noticed the back-and-forth snark between the teenaged Vivian and JoLynne. They were kids, too. They hadn't known how to appreciate what they had in that moment.

God, if only.

She ran her fingers over the words on the headstone. They were worn now, softened by weather and time. Had he lived, her little brother would now be in his fifties! How was it possible that so much time had passed? So much was lost.

It made her want to grab onto everything remaining with both hands and maybe her teeth.

She placed the flowers gently at the base of the stone, stood, and brushed dirt from her knees. Beau slipped his arm around her shoulders, and she leaned into him, struggling not to cry.

They lingered a while longer, saying nothing. The wind shimmered through the cottonwoods, the leaves whispering.

Beau kissed her on the temple. "I'm sorry, babe, but we should get going."

"I know."

"You okay?"

She looked up at him. "I feel guilty and sad—of course I do. I have ever since it happened. Vivian, too. But just now, I had this feeling, not exactly like Josh talking to me, but like I finally understood. Even though it hurts to walk away, I still have a life. I get to live, Beau."

Tears slipped down her cheeks, and he wiped them away with his free hand.

"It feels like freedom. A blessing. And it's still horrible. But I can't waste it."

"We won't," he said, pulling her into a full-body hug that secured her to the earth.

Twenty-Nine

The wind teased the edge of JoLynne's sleeve as she leaned her elbow out the passenger window. She breathed in the late-October air: dust and juniper, sagebrush, and the faint, sweet smell of hay. Overhead, the sky was the color of warm denim, faded at the edges, stitched with gulls.

Beau turned off the lane and drove up the driveway toward Nate's house, and beyond it, the one he no longer occupied. Signs of improvement showed up subtly. The rural mailbox no longer listed sideways, and the derelict car in front of Nate's house was gone. A flowerbed had appeared near the porch, the colorful foxglove and zinnias hinting at the presence of a woman.

A young man clearing weeds stopped to look at them. A wheelbarrow half-filled with straw sat by the barn, and a girl of about twelve was scrubbing a water trough with a stiff brush, her sleeves pushed to her elbows.

Parking beside Nate's truck, Beau killed the motor. "The place looks busy."

"Who are those kids?" JoLynne asked.

"Our renters." Beau unsnapped his seatbelt. "Let's find Nate, and I'll introduce you."

They scuffed through the dirt to Nate's house. The screen door opened, and a woman stepped out.

JoLynne had to blink to make sure she was seeing right.

It was Vera, Leonard's daughter. She wore cutoffs, a bright tee shirt, and a faded pair of Vans. Her smile was bright and warm. "Hey, you guys! Are you here to go riding?" She trotted down the steps.

"We hadn't planned on it." JoLynne swung her finger between Vera and the house. "So, you and Nate?"

"Looks like it," said Vera, sticking her hands in her back pockets. "After the fair, we went for a walk on the beach…"

"And the rest is history," said Nate, coming toward them from the barn. He stood next to Vera, who leaned a little, pressing against him gently. He slipped his arm around her waist.

Beau looked down at the ground, shaking his head and smiling.

"Good for you guys," said JoLynne. "So, who're the kids?"

"They live here now," said Beau. "Remember I told you about that family living in their van?" He lifted his chin at his brother. "Nate rescued them."

"Yeah, I guess," said Nate. "A few weeks after they bombed the interview, the mom came back with her younger brother, that boy clearing weeds. Said the husband was out of the picture, and they'd work real hard if we'd let them stay."

Vera smiled up at him. "He told them only the older ones. He wasn't going to have child labor around here."

"Still, they cleaned the place top to bottom," Nate said. "They can't do enough. I think they're just so relieved to be here."

JoLynne glanced over at the young girl. "What about the husband? Will he make trouble?"

"He steps foot on the property," said Nate, "he'll have to deal with me."

"And me." Vera looped her arm through his.

"Are you living here, too?"

"For now," she said, smiling up at Nate.

"For good," he said, pecking her on the lips.

"Awww," said JoLynne, and they all laughed.

Beau nudged her gently. "Want to go say hi to the horses?"

"You know me," she said.

They said their goodbyes and wandered toward the back pasture, where Buck, Shorty, and Hashtag stood idly swishing their tails in the shade of a giant sycamore.

JoLynne walked close to Beau, their steps matching, the silence comfortable. She inhaled deeply, the fragrance of pepper trees and eucalyptus filling her lungs. Making her happy. She'd spent most of the week driving folks around to doctor's appointments, grocery runs, even an airport pickup for the new volunteer at Teresa's clinic, but today was theirs.

"I like it here," she said softly. "I hope that family gets to stay."

"They can if they want to," he said. "They're safe now."

They stopped at the fence rail in the shade, resting their elbows on the wood and watching the horses. Overhead, JoLynne spotted a pair of red-tailed hawks circling each other. "Vera finally found a place where she fits."

"Yeah, the two of them—they're perfect for each other."

"Do you ever think about how you and I almost blew it?"

Beau didn't answer right away.

"I do," he said finally. "I think about how it seemed logical to run."

"But we didn't."

"We almost did." He nudged her playfully. "Little Ms. Independent here."

She gave him a wry smile. "And Mister Co—"

"Don't even say it." He grabbed her in a hug, kissing her fully so that she couldn't finish the sentence.

When they broke apart, she rested her head on his shoulder, content.

Beau still had his rental in town, but he lived with her now. Last week, they'd painted the kitchen and replaced the old table with something new and solid, something that felt like both of them. Most evenings, they walked the beach after dinner, sometimes talking, sometimes not. They were settling in.

With Selina proving to be a reliable second-in-command, Beau was finally getting the hang of delegating. His days were smoother, his stress lower. Life was easier now. Not perfect, but easier.

Now, they leaned on the gate side by side, watching Hashtag sniff curiously at a patch of thistle, only to sneeze violently and then look puzzled.

"Stupid pony," said Beau.

"Smart enough to have his own social media account, though." After the fair, Cass had insisted, and it was possible the pony would be making appearances at other events.

JoLynne laughed to herself. Life was pretty sweet.

They stayed like that for a while, sunlight warming the pasture, the smell of cut grass reaching them on the wind. A screen door slammed, followed by a child's voice yelling, "Levi, Mom made chocolate chip cookies!"

JoLynne grinned. "We should go introduce ourselves."

"Think that's too conniving?"

"There's cookies."

He tucked her arm through his. "Let's go say hello."

As they walked back toward Beau's old house, one of the horses whinnied, and she looked out across the pasture one last time.

Years ago, a photograph had caught her in a moment of freedom she didn't know how to hold on to. But here, now—sun-warmed, windblown, hand in hand with a man who belonged in her future—she'd found it again.

Not in a picture, but in real time.

And this time, she wasn't riding alone.

Thirty

Epilogue

Three Months Later

Two of the three barrels were down. Once again, they'd started too tight and had come out of the turn wide. JoLynne pulled Jessabelle up, the mare flinging her head in protest as they slowed. For an older horse, she still had lots of fire.

"Sorry, girl," JoLynne soothed. "That one's on me." She reached forward and patted Jessie's neck where the muscles bunched and twitched under her skin. The mare was hot, focused, and ready to go again.

Beau stood outside the corral with one boot propped on the lower rail, arms folded. His expression was half admiring, half anxious. Vivian sat on the top fence rail beside him like a twelve-year-old.

JoLynne trotted over and pulled Jessie to a walk. "What'd you think?"

"You're crowding her pocket on the first turn." Beau pushed back his Stetson. "Need to give her more room to pivot clean."

"I felt that, too. She had to scramble.

Vivian squinted at Beau. "Did you used to compete?"

"Not me. My daughter ran barrels all four years of high school."

"A girl after my own heart," said JoLynne. "Vivian and I never missed a rodeo back in the day."

"Really." Beau turned to look up at Viv. "What'd you compete in?"

"Beauty pageant." Vivian wiped her hands on her jeans. "I still can't believe you signed up for this," she said to JoLynne. "You two were supposed to go to the fair to watch. Eat kettle corn. Judge other people."

"It wasn't the plan, but I just want to feel the thrill again, you know?" JoLynne nudged Jessie back toward the barrels. "Let's take it from the top."

Beau tapped the timer on his phone. "Ready."

JoLynne kneed Jessabelle, and she took off like a bullet, weaving around the three barrels and then racing back the length of the arena before pulling up to a stop. "How was that?" she asked, both she and the horse breathing hard.

"Better." Beau checked his phone. "But you need to shave it some more."

"She's already flyin'," said Vivian, shaking her head. "This is flat-ass crazy."

"I'll be fine. She's a great horse. Experienced and smart." At seventeen, Jessie was on the outer edge of competitive barrel racing, but JoLynne wanted to give the veteran mare a chance to relive her glory days. "She's got such fire, I can feel it. She wants to run, wants to compete."

"Projecting much?" Viv climbed down off the rail. "I need to get home. You two have fun. And Sis? Try not to fall off."

"You got it." JoLynne turned to Beau. "This little gal remembers, though. Did you see?"

"She's a real pro," he said. "Why don't you walk her a bit, and I'll meet you at the barn to get her settled."

JoLynne clucked at the mare and began cooling her down. She appreciated his support. It wasn't something she'd been sure of when she first mentioned the event. He had raised an eyebrow, but then, seeing her shoulders slump a little, changed his stance. "It's not like you're going on the road for a rodeo career. At least try it once," he'd said.

"Once, sure," JoLynne had laughed. "You only have to break your neck one time."

He'd smiled at her, as if seeing right through the fear to the competitive horsewoman in her soul.

"Alright then. I'm going to sign up." And she had.

That was back in the summer. Now, it was October, and the rodeo was tomorrow.

Out on her patio, the aroma of barbecue mingled with the scent of fall in the air. Beau stood at the grill, tongs in one hand, ready to flip the steaks. "Three minutes," he hollered.

JoLynne pushed the slider open with her hip and carried out a serving tray with baked potatoes, sautéed spinach, and condiments.

The sun had just kissed the horizon, turning the sky peach and lavender. Out in the darkening water, a few surfers bobbed in wetsuits, chasing one more wave before the light gave out. Setting down her tray, JoLynne wrapped her arms around Beau from behind, resting her cheek between his shoulder blades as the waves pounded the sand in the distance.

With his free hand, Beau covered hers. "Love you, babe."

She sighed, feeling the same way, although it was hard for her to say it. Since he'd moved in, their attachment had only deepened. The house was feeling more like theirs than hers, and she was happy about that. Beau's boots were by the door now, his sweatshirt on the hook. His toothbrush in the cup next to hers. Every weeknight when he came home from work, their dinners were intimate and heartfelt, whether here in their cozy home, in town, or somewhere overlooking the beach. Sometimes on the weekends they'd join other friends for a meal, and pool parties were becoming a regular attraction.

He slid the steaks onto their plates. "Are you nervous about tomorrow?"

"Only every second." She unwrapped the foil from their baked potatoes.

Beau sat down. "Jessie will do well. She's more than ready to get back out there."

"I hope I am."

"What I saw out there today? The two of you are old pros. You've got muscle memory, and so does she."

"Emphasis on old." She looked up and smiled at him to show she was kidding. Because JoLynne didn't feel old. She felt stronger than ever. After all she'd been through, look at her now: a new man in her life, an old, beloved sport, and a sweet horse. What else was there?

Beau reached across the table and took her hand. His fingers were rough, warm, and familiar. "You'll win."

"I don't so much care about that as not getting hurt. Me or Jessie."

Beau cut into his steak and took a bite, chewed for a while, looking thoughtful. Then, with a sidelong glance, he said, "You know, you could sleep in tomorrow. Blow off the rodeo and go walking on the beach with me."

JoLynne didn't look up from her plate. "I know."

"No shame in deciding you've already proved your point."

"What point is that?"

"That you're brave. That you're a damn fine horsewoman. That Jessabelle is lucky you found her."

JoLynne set her fork down. "That's not the point."

"No?"

She looked out toward the dark water, where the surf was barely visible now, a low hum beneath the clink of their silverware. Then she turned to him.

"I've had so many second acts, Beau. Reinventions, recoveries. You've seen it. You've lived it. But this time, this one's just for me. Okay, and maybe the horse." She held out her wineglass, and he got up and topped it off.

"I signed up for this competition because I want to feel fast again," she said. "Dominant and a little wild. I want to do something that scares the crap out of me and succeed."

Beau stared at her across the table, his expression unreadable.

"And if I fall on my butt," she added, "you can pick me up, dust me off, and take me out for a nice meal."

"You'll be fine." He grinned. "You don't need me to tell you that. You know it in your bones."

"I do." She tipped her glass toward him. "Tomorrow, we're going to win. Or at least not embarrass ourselves."

She hoped.

Jessabelle fought the reins and tossed her head. The noise from the arena thundered like a freight train, with the crowd yelling and the loudspeaker squawking. The horse danced in tight circles, nostrils flared, wanting to run. "Easy, girl," JoLynne soothed, her voice quiet and the reins held low.

Beau stood nearby. He'd helped them unload and get to the gate, his calm presence settling Jessabelle and JoLynne both. He was always reassuring, shoring up her confidence when it dipped.

Even this morning, on the way to the San Diego Fairgrounds, the horse munching hay in the trailer behind Beau's truck, JoLynne wasn't done venting her fears.

What if Jessie freaks out?

What if I break something?

What if, if, if...

"I can turn this rig around," he said. "You have nothing to prove."

"Except to myself," she muttered.

Overhead, the announcer's voice crackled through a too-loud speaker, reminding people to get their snacks and hurry back to their seats for the last competitor in the senior women's barrel racing event. The first five had done well, with one scary wobble that had the spectators gasp as one. But the woman had stayed aboard, even though she'd knocked down two of the three barrels.

"Alright, folks, next up in the Silver Stars class, we've got JoLynne Coltrane, riding a rescue named Jessabelle."

Jess's hooves raked the dirt, her skin rippling, electric. She blew hard through her nostrils, a short warning burst.

"Easy now," JoLynne said, steady and low. "We've done this."

"Ladies and gents, Jessabelle and her rider are both experienced competitors, but it's been a while. Let's see if they've still got it."

A chuckle rippled through the audience.

"Ms. Coltrane told us she's here to have fun, and we're all rooting for her. And just in case, we've got the oxygen tanks ready down at the first aid tent!"

The crowd laughed. Jessabelle danced, and JoLynne reined her around, keeping the horse on track. She had no time to worry about fools. It was time to line up and fire away.

"We're going!" she shouted to Beau.

"Turn and burn, baby!" he called back.

She tapped her heels against Jessie's flanks and the mare shot forward, thundering down the alley toward the light and roar of the arena. Bursting through the gate, they flew toward the first barrel, taking too long to get there and circling wide.

The second barrel came fast. Jess was amped, cut close, and JoLynne's calf brushed it. The barrel wobbled but didn't fall.

Launching Jess toward the third, the noise in the arena seemed to fade, and it was as if time had slowed. JoLynne felt every breath pulled in and shoved out, every muscle tensing and releasing, the horse's mane lashing her face as JoLynne bent close, rounding the last barrel.

And then the crowd erupted as Jessabelle turned toward home. "GO, GO, GO!" JoLynne screamed, practically levitating over the saddle as Jess thundered toward the finish line.

And then it was done.

JoLynne sat back hard, heels down, Jessabelle resisting at first until she saw the wall coming up and hit the brakes. They circled twice, both of them riding the last surge of adrenaline, lungs heaving, sweat and dust hanging in the air.

Behind them, the announcer's voice blared over the loudspeakers, fighting to be heard over the roar of the crowd.

"And that was JoLynne Coltrane aboard Jessabelle! Final time — twenty point one-three seconds! Folks, that's a great finish, earning our rider second place in the Silver Stars division!"

Applause rolled through the arena as JoLynne guided Jessabelle into the victory loop, joining the first and third place finishers as they made a joyful circuit, waving to the cheering stands. This was the best, the very best. It all came back, those happy days when she'd won trophies in high school, when her family would cheer her from the stands.

She leaned forward, smiling so big her face hurt, and patted the mare's neck.

"Good girl," she murmured. "You did it, you gorgeous, wild thing."

Sweat slicked Jessabelle's mane. Her ears flicked back and forth, muscles coiled, still ready to run if asked.

Blinking against the sunlight, JoLynne lifted her gaze to the stands. Vivian was on her feet, waving and whistling, two fingers jammed in her mouth the way Dad had taught them. Beside her stood Beau.

Their eyes met. He tapped his chest, over his heart. JoLynne smiled and nudged Jessabelle forward. As she reined up near the rail, Beau slung one leg over the barrier and swung down to the arena floor, landing lightly beside her. Then he lifted a single red rose.

She shifted forward in the saddle and leaned down, the leather creaking softly as she reached for the flower. Beau caught her hand and held it, drawing her close. His lips found hers, and for a moment the roar of the crowd fell away.

"I love you, too," she said, smiling against his mouth.

In response, the intensity of his kiss told her everything she needed to know. She was glad to have said it. Glad to have taken a chance on this day, on this man.

A wolf-whistle shrilled from the announcer's booth, and Jessabelle shifted, pulling them apart. JoLynne lifted the rose in a quick salute to the audience, then handed Beau the reins as they turned toward the tunnel, yielding the arena to the first-place rider.

She slid down from the saddle, legs a little shaky now that the adrenaline was ebbing, and let Beau catch her. He wrapped his arms around her, and she kissed him again, softer now, a chapter closed, a new one opening in its place. She rested her forehead against his chest.

"Next time," he said, "you'll be the winner."

JoLynne leaned back and looked up at him, smiling. "I already am."

The End
Thank you for reading! It's been a ride, hasn't it?

Afterword

Would you like to know what happens next with JoLynne and Beau? To get your free bonus epilogue ebook, *Valentine's Day in Serena Cove,* go to **SilverRomanceBooks.net/free-books** and click on *Valentine's Day.* If you're in a place where you can't click (like you're reading this in paperback), just go to SilverRomanceBooks.net and click on the Free-Books page.

I hope you enjoyed getting to know the characters in Serena Cove. If so, I'd really appreciate it if you'd leave a review. It can be short! Just tell Amazon you loved the book, that it was nice to read a story about midlifers, and that you'd like to see more from this author. That's it! Reviews like yours help other readers find their next enjoyable read—and hopefully, their favorite new author!

To see all my books or join my newsletter group for updates and deals, go to SilverRomanceBooks.net. Let's stay in touch!

Lynne M. Spreen

Acknowledgements

Writing a book is such a big job! By the time you get to the end of it, you forget some important bits, mess up the timeline, or don't even notice how many times you repeat a certain phrase. My favorites, apparently, are "Me, too," "Me, neither," and "My god." (No, it shouldn't be capitalized unless you're referring to Him specifically. Thank you for noticing, though. If you'd like to join my pre-publication group, let me know. I'm always eager to find sharp-eyed readers who notice things in my new books before they go out. Contact me at **Lynne@SilverRomanceBooks.net** if you'd like to receive free, advance copies.)

Many thanks to all the wonderful people who helped me with this book starting with my editor Sarah Lamb and beta reader Brooke De Lira, both of whom helped shape and polish this work into something fun and enjoyable for my readers.

Thanks to my coaches and colleagues at Best Page Forward. I'm grateful for your guidance and companionship.

But most of all, to my sweet husband, Bill, who makes me feel like the smartest and most talented person on the planet. I love you, honey. Here's to another thirty years.

Made in United States
Cleveland, OH
09 April 2026

35589569R00125